I0538874

London Fell is a widely-published author of political and legal thought issues over a series of 12 books. His newfound literary works are now being produced over a number of individual books. He is a graduate of Princeton University and holds a doctoral degree from Columbia University. In his post-retirement years his interests have continued to develop in novels, poetry and plays.

To Alexander and Jason, my sons and helpers.

London Fell

CLAUDETTE MONET IN AMERICA

(First Novel in O.A Trilogy)

AUSTIN MACAULEY PUBLISHERS™

LONDON • CAMBRIDGE • NEW YORK • SHARJAH

Ordering Information:
Quantity sales: special discounts are available on quantity purchases by corporations, associations, and others. For details, contact the publisher at the address below.

Publisher's Cataloguing-in-Publication data
Fell, London
Claudette Monet in America

ISBN 9781641823982 (Paperback)
ISBN 9781641823999 (Hardback)
ISBN 9781641824002 (E-Book)

The main category of the book — Fiction / Historical

www.austinmacauley.com

First Published (2018)
Austin Macauley Publishers LLC.
40 Wall Street, 28th Floor
New York, NY 10005
USA

mail-usa@austinmacauley.com
+1 (646) 5125767

Table of Contents

Prefatory

These impressionistic "fantasy sketches" of "*Claudette Monet in America*" center on her as namesake of French painter Claude Monet—the legendary master of that genre in art.

In the realm of the imagination, all things become possible. Flights of fantasy can merge with the rush of historical events. The world of the past comes alive in the present. Past scenes give luster to their present settings, which in turn furnish lenses for viewing the past. Past and present merge in the realm of fantasy. If complex, the story can be fathomed through straightforward exposition, narration, or description. A willing suspension of disbelief can help the story become compelling as well as authentic.

Such liberties, when taken in a short historical fantasy novel or novella, can take various forms, while maintaining historical authenticity. If a profile sketch of the protagonist forms the broad centerpiece, surrounding matters may be left sketchier. Scenes with elusive or shadowy "impressions" can be left that way, not filled in with further details as found in a fuller account. To keep the main Monet plot moving along, within its own "painterly" contours, can become a kind of fleeting intrigue *rapide* or *schnelles* spiel.

Many questions arise. How might a Monet artist like our Claudette have viewed and experienced American scenes back then and later on? How might she fit in there—or not? Would glimpses open up into her inner self and its conflicts? How would other people fit in around her? How would the great legacy of Claude Monet, who never came to America, have treated Claudette Monet, who did so before the end of his life in 1926? Would darker configurations of race, nationality, sex, and crime, as of family and love, lie below the bright serene surfaces of her impressionist dream world? Any issues for today?

Part One: France

1. Discovering an Identity

They are there, still, in a pleasant Normandy village outside Paris, close enough to the city with its vibrant gathering places for artists and intellectuals, yet sufficiently removed to a world of natural beauty all its own. There, tranquil, have long flourished his celebrated Giverny residence, gardens, and tree-lined pond with its iconic bridge. This central figure of Impressionist painting, Claude Monet, is venerated, still, in his scenic abode downstream west from Paris along the River Seine in northwestern France. The Master's legendary Giverny aura gave rise to an extended art colony and welcomes, still, its flocks of visitors and pilgrims.

There, Claude Monet gathered around him extended arrangements of natural scenery for him and select others to portray and for extended groupings of family and friends to share in the community. In his later years in the early twentieth century, Monet became increasingly absorbed in his Giverny world—in large measure because advancing age and declining eyesight made him a willing prisoner. With growing reliance there on different kinds of helpers, he was not always acutely aware of the clusters of people around him. From 1912—or even earlier—to 1923, before his cataract operation, Monet's increasingly blurred and cloudy vision not only affected his perception of form, color, and light but also limited his view of people and surroundings. He spoke about this.

Meanwhile, by the 1920s, in the final decade of his life, some critics declared the style of Impressionist painting Monet had championed *passé,* over the hill, in the post–war era of newer, more avant-garde styles of art and thought. But the name and career of Claude Monet remained a central touchstone for his many faithful followers. For those who made pilgrimages to Giverny, or who sought the cachet of the Monet name in furtherance of their own artistic careers, the great master and his circle were still in vogue. Still others would come to see in Monet's later paintings, especially those of water lilies, an abstract vision ahead of its time.

One can easily imagine how an impressionable young woman like Claudette and her ambitious mother Eugènie could have been captivated by the artistic and social aura of Claude Monet's Giverny, where they occasionally visited. By 1900 when Claudette was born not long after her parents' marriage, the Monet name was already legendary.

So captivated, in fact, was Eugènie that after she divorced her American husband—with the unpromising name of Jack Hornsby—she adopted for herself and her daughter the surname Monet. She claimed, or invented, the prior patrimony of a long-lost cousin by that name. To make the name-recognition for her daughter complete, Eugènie also gave her the first name Claudette. Did this name change give Claudette, much less her mother, greater entrée into the French artistic–social world, beyond a greater feeling of belonging? That remained open to question. But it certainly helped advance Claudette's artistic career when she went to the United States in the 1920s. There the name Claudette Monet would be seen as an unquestionable link to Claude Monet.

• • •

Even so, the whole business was tenuous and bound to produce in Claudette a complex personality, for she was never altogether sure of her own identity and continually felt somewhat *déclassée*. Once Claudette was old enough to ask her mother questions about herself, her past, and even her future, she soon began asking more difficult, even troubling, questions.

"Mother, where is my father? Why doesn't he ever see me or you? It's as though he just left us— because he doesn't love us anymore."

"Well," Eugènie started to reply...

"And why did you change our names from Hornsby to Monet and mine from Clarissa to Claudette? Or did he do it? Not everyone is comfortable with that."

Again, Eugènie would usually hesitate, and Claudette would leave unasked further questions like, "Why do people sometimes still ask me about all that?"

"It's difficult for me, too, to think about your father. I had to divorce him when you were very young. I had to change who I was and drop my married name. I'm sure it must have been hard for you, too, to have your father leave us without a trace and go back to America. That's why I had no choice but to get a divorce."

"Where did he go in America?"

"I suppose to the northeast where he came from. He talked about New York, New Jersey, and Pennsylvania."

"I still have dreams about all this," Claudette would sometimes say. "Daddy sometimes calls out to me as 'little Clair.'"

Her mother would respond offhandedly at times. Or she would change the subject by adding: "I have *dreams* for *you*, dear, that you will develop your own identity, as I tried to do for myself and for you. Your artistic talents are already beginning to show, and they are far better than mine. I hope you will pursue them. Your name will open doors for you. I have great hope for you, dear." Claudette would usually stop to ponder *that*.

At other times, the exchanges would not progress as well. For instance: "Are you sure I'm not illegitimate?" Or: "I need to see my father, not just in my dreams."

As Claudette grew into young adulthood, her complex personality was becoming more evident. A crisis of identity was increasingly apparent. More and more she sought solace

15

in her art, even with an *eye* to the lands of her father in America. What *would* a Monet eye there see—and seek to capture?

• • •

Despite bearing the name of the late French empress, Eugènie Hornsby (maiden name Desmoulins) came of solid *petit bourgeois* stock. Her parents and, indeed, her forbears for several generations operated a patisserie in Montmartre that brought in a tidy, if not extravagant, income. Eugènie might well have grown up to inherit this had it not been for the day (Eugènie was eleven) when her mother awoke to the smell of burning croissants and found that she had no husband and an oven full of charred pastry. Georges Desmoulins had decamped with the pretty maid of a local family with whom he removed to a distant city. At least he had the grace never to show himself again.

There was little about those in Eugènie's family that might be called attractive, and Eugènie herself was no exception. Her two good features were her clear cornflower-blue eyes and her thick dirty-blonde hair, but they were about all to note. She was short, and her figure was podgy, with no waist to speak of. She also had a pronounced overbite, in consequence of which she spoke with a slight lisp. It was only to be expected that she had few suitors. So when tall, elegant Jack Hornsby came courting—Jack Hornsby of the slender physique and sunny smile...to say nothing of the extravagant plans (or perhaps just hopes) for an affluent future, Eugènie was only too willing to grant him what he so clearly wanted.

• • •

And when Eugènie soon discovered that she was pregnant, Jack did what all concerned considered the honorable thing and married her—so expeditiously that Claudette could plausibly have arrived a bit prematurely to a

16

matron who had brought her virginity to the nuptial bed. Once Claudette had become a definite presence, however, Eugènie discovered that her husband had little interest in child rearing—and no intention of letting his daughter's needs tie him down. His absences from home became more and more protracted until at the end, he simply disappeared.

Growing up in Montmartre, Eugènie had spent her life so surrounded by artists that she became quite *blasé* about them. Starving artists frequently offered her parents paintings in exchange for pastries; but, wisely or foolishly, the Desmoulins had a firm policy never to accept the proffered art, although they sometimes wavered on this. A case in point was a sunny canvas depicting Notre Dame Cathedral that Claude Monet offered them at a low point in his life, a time when he was desperate to feed his ailing young wife Camille. The Desmoulins wavered for several days, but in the end they declined to accept it. The painting was later shown at a major exposition and sold for thousands of francs to a wealthy American. The history of this gaffe was something Mme. Desmoulins lamented repeatedly to her daughter but never revealed to outsiders.

So with his enormous success—and the enormous wealth it earned him—Claude Monet became for Eugènie the *beau idéal* of artistic achievement. When her daughter later came along, there was little hesitation in her decision to name, or rename, her Claudette, after her husband's departure, in place of the name Clarissa he had chosen in honor of his mother.

• • •

The child of Eugènie and Jack was fortunate to inherit the best features of both her parents. From her mother she got thick blonde hair, the kind that she had only to brush for it to fall into place in an attractive coif. From both parents she took her blue eyes, but hers were more the cornflower blue of her mother's than the ice blue of Jack Hornsby's. From her father she inherited a tall, slender silhouette. By

17

the time she was twelve years old, she was as tall as her mother; by sixteen, she was a head taller. She also had the same perfect teeth coupled with a smile that was like the sunrise.

2. French Connections

Claudette's mother Eugènie had her own inner demons. To name, or rename, her daughter so closely after a great artist required a remarkable leap of the imagination, if not a downright twisted sense of reality. "I did it to help give you an instant name-recognition in the art world and in wider public circles," she told her daughter. In fact, the *cachet* would come to Eugènie herself as well, or so she felt. "I want what's best for you. To advance in a career dominated by men you need an *entrée* in order to be successful."

Yet Eugènie was also looking for her own *entrée* into the Parisian artistic–social worlds and their satellites at places like Monet's Giverny. She had seen and felt firsthand the aura of success on exhibit there and wanted somehow to share in it for herself as well as her daughter. For, to be blunt, Eugènie had been a failed artist in her younger years. "I want you to succeed where I have failed," she would tell Claudette. "Giverny is my idea of success." She would sometimes add: "I know firsthand the feelings of rejection we suffer at places like Giverny, where large extended families and relationships among artists seem to be completely closed to outsiders and would-be artists. But I am only ambitious for you, my dear."

With her American husband Jack Hornsby as an awkward albatross around her neck, Eugènie had quickly found the close-knit, interconnected intellectual and social worlds of Paris at the dawning of the twentieth century difficult to access. To gain acceptance she was willing to take bold steps. Multiple affairs with influential men and

19

occasionally women—had not helped her advancement in the ways she had hoped. Doubts began to be raised about the legitimacy of her daughter. Who was the real father? Was it Jack Hornsby or someone else? The circumstances surrounding his definitive departure from France and subsequent disappearance in America were, for mother as well as daughter, a source of uncertainty and anxiety. Eugènie's own insecurities were reflected in those of her daughter's. All of which added to the confusion and mystery over names.

"I suppose," Eugènie once confided to a close friend, "I have had a princess complex. My name in French society has often been associated with women of position and fashion, like the noted wife of Emperor Napoleon III after whom I was named, Empress Eugènie. Not to overlook that name in the title of a novel by Balzac. My parents felt that giving me such a promising name would help me along in life through a kind of name-recognition. Perhaps that helps explain my choice of names for my daughter."

Parental patterns had taken, and were taking, their toll. "I had no choice," Eugènie again confided, "but to divorce Jack after he walked out on us. He didn't fit in over here; but I wanted to keep the marriage for the sake of the child. It was very distressing for the little girl when her papa finally left her for good."

"Why did he leave you?" Eugènie's friend asked.

"He didn't like France, didn't speak much French, at least not acceptably. He didn't like my sense of self-advancement. He wasn't very successful in what he did, which was some kind of business that had nothing to do with the artistic and social worlds over here."

"Tell me, Eugènie, what were your parents like? Was it a happy family?"

"Not really. My father left my mother and me for another woman and moved far away."

"What then?"

"Well, I resolved to find my own way in life. I told myself I'd never depend on a husband or any other people."

"But then you've had many affairs and relationships. Were those all meant to help achieve your goals?"

"Yes. So in the end I behaved just like my parents in ways that led to my own failed marriage. I hope Claudette, if and when she marries, will not repeat my mistakes but find herself better than I found myself."

"Amen," said the friend.

"Let not the sins of the parents be visited upon their children," added Eugènie.

"Why did you wait so long to tell me all this?" Eugènie's daughter eventually asked. "Or were you planning to hold back until I became suspicious and pressed you for the truth? Is there still more to tell?"

For Eugènie, reality was stranger than fiction. Her French connections in the late nineteenth and early twentieth centuries presented a compelling story in itself. From her younger years, with marriage to Jack Hornsby and birth of Claudette around 1900, on into World War I, Eugènie was buffeted by many turn-of-the-century forces. They fed into her conflicted nature and that of the child.

• • •

Until she was about twelve, Claudette thought her mother immutable and infallible, a combination of God and the Rock of Gibraltar, the source of all knowledge and her moral center. But as she arrived at adolescence, she began to see the world with eyes that compared and evaluated what they saw and to form opinions of her own. She saw that Eugènie despite her talk about the need to be *chic,* slender, sabotaged her own efforts to achieve her goal. Her waistline never shrank to the twenty-five inches she desired—largely because she could never resist one more pastry or another brandy. And in an age when women were expected to be dressed up, she somehow managed always to fall short. The sash she wore with a green dress clashed rather than vibrating; the once-elegant fur collar on her coat bore too clearly evidence that a family of moths had dined there. The

21

carefully crafted coiffure perpetually wilted to one side and threatened to collapse entirely if she became excited.

Claudette realized that when Eugènie looked into the mirror, she saw her fantasy image of herself rather than the imperfect creature her daughter was beginning to discern.

Then Claudette began to make sense of the many liaisons with men Eugènie had formed over the years. Claudette had become accustomed to being packed off to Grandmother Desmoulins's at a moment's notice because mother had a project in the works, often a sudden trip to the countryside (in the company of an artist somewhat better-known than she) to practice painting *en plein air*. The scales ultimately dropped from Claudette's eyes in the aftermath of a particular affair.

• • •

Mamoud Faood (a man of indeterminate Near Eastern origin) was the owner of a small, ill-lit gallery that showed the work of a succession of artists who never achieved anything resembling success. From time to time, Eugènie and Claudette attended an opening there to munch stale *petits fours*, swill cheap wine, and make fun of the art on display.

But suddenly M. Faood became part of their family. He escorted Eugènie all over Paris and out into the country. Claudette was frequently packed off to *grandmère's* house (she had long since figured out the significance of this) but found it confusing that her mother evidently did not like M. Faood. She called him "the Levantine"; and when his name came up in conversation, she would further badmouth him under her breath.

Eugènie's purpose became clear to Claudette one afternoon when she returned from school to find her mother in agitated elation. "Oh, my dear," she said gathering Claudette into an uncommon embrace, "you'll never guess. M. Faood is going to give me a show. The artist he had lined up for next month has pulled out, and he offered it to me."

"How wonderful!" said Claudette and cringed inwardly. She guessed (accurately, as it turned out) how irrational Eugènie would be until the opening.

And indeed the next month was hellish as Eugènie put the finishing touches on several dozen canvases, only to reject half of them once they were ready and to start a few new paintings that the press of time forced her to abandon. Finally, M. Faood collected as many pictures as his gallery would hold and declared the exhibit selected. Thereupon Eugènie focused her anxiety on selecting a gown for the opening. At one point or another, she chose most of the dresses in her wardrobe and made modest alterations to seven or eight of them.

When the show had been hung, there was still one small corner that lacked art. In a fit of generosity (or maternal pride), Eugènie offered her daughter the chance to hang two of her little watercolors. Claudette accepted with a bit of reluctance.

The show was a fiasco. Barely a dozen people came to the opening, and in the end only two of Eugènie's paintings were sold—one of them to her mother. Both of Claudette's watercolors were snapped up at the opening.

Once the dust settled, Eugènie decided that Claudette was clearly the gifted one in the family and turned her attention to nurturing her daughter's talent.

M. Faood disappeared permanently from their lives.

3. Parisian Life

By the late nineteenth and early twentieth centuries, Parisian life was, in fact, becoming more open to change and responsive to new forces, more dynamic than Eugènie's perceptions and personality would allow her to grasp. These trends would accelerate after World War I—which wiped out *la belle epoque*. Among the most dynamic of these changes was the growing influx of foreigners, who lent an air of new mobility and new possibilities. For one thing, Americans were flocking more and more to Paris. It was in this broader context that Jack Hornsby found himself there and eventually married to Eugènie, just before 1900. He found her living as much in the past as in the present. Another influx there was of citizens from France's colonies in places like Africa, most notably Morocco or, as it was sometimes called, French Morocco. In that context, Claudette was to meet Dominique, better known to her closer friends as simply Monique. Their new relationship would become a vital influence in the life of Claudette Monet—whose name Dominique did not question at all but fully accepted.

In the early 1900s—prior to World War I—Parisian life increasingly took changing currents in the artistic and social worlds, even for people on the periphery like Eugènie and Claudette.

Decades earlier, Napoleon III and his urban planner, Baron Haussmann, had cleared away large areas of Paris to make way for broad boulevards in hopes of making it the most beautiful city in Europe. As a result, the Montmartre district had been growing in size and density as displaced people moved there. Now adding to their ranks were all sorts of newcomers. Old and new elements created vibrant mixes in intellectual, artistic, and social life. The more traditional styles of Monet and his fellow Impressionists were still a focal point through their gallery exhibitions. Now added were avant-garde styles such as Picasso's and Braque's Cubism. These were exhibited in galleries as well as in collections centered around wealthy American-born Gertrude Stein and her family.

For Eugènie, Claudette, and their friends, the choices were still clear. The more genteel pretty world of Monet and the Impressionists remained preferable to the harsh jarring depictions of such artists as Picasso, Braque, and the other Cubists. And yet, such fractured viewpoints could seem more akin to the unsettled, conflicted outlooks of Eugènie and Claudette than the serenity of their seeming opposite. Or were the Impressionists and their world simply more soothing?

The traumas of the Great War brought both of these art worlds to their knees as France entered a very dark period, especially on the eastern front through German inroads on French soil. The aging Monet seldom exhibited his works in the Parisian galleries and spent more time at his Giverny home. This circumstance gave Eugènie and Claudette freer opening to flaunt the cachet of the Monet name in Paris and its environs.

Meanwhile, wartime austerities forced their own setbacks on the more Modernist styles fostered by Gertrude Stein and others who shared her taste for the avant-garde.

With the coming of peace in 1918, the disruptions of war began to fade into memory. By the 1920s, the diverging art worlds of Monet and Picasso could sometimes seem complementary amid the multifaceted cultural resurgence in France following the upheavals of the Great War. Although Monet was slowly losing his sight, his Giverny world had not lost its attraction and was rebounding as he spent ever more time there. Impressionism's allure had spread to America. As Americans flocked to Paris, American

25

influences were growing in France. Abstraction was finding its way across a broad spectrum. The patronage of Gertrude Stein and family was rebounding somewhat on a wide front. Much later, the abstractions of Picasso and Monet would be well-juxtaposed, agitated versus peaceful, in New York's Museum of Modern Art.

• • •

As one of those other people flocking to Paris during this period from Morocco, France's colonial outpost in northwestern Africa, Dominique Dupré had a curious, sometimes conflicted past of her own. Born, like Claudette, at the turn of the century, Dominique came to Paris shortly after the War. She sought art and acceptance in another cosmopolitan city like her native Casablanca—the largest city in Morocco and situated on the Atlantic Coast just south of Gibraltar. There, her (white) French father, like Jack Hornsby, had left her and her (half-black) mother. Since blacks were, and have been, conspicuously absent from the Arabic-speaking countries across northern Africa, the Duprés mixed marriage had sometimes left them feeling like outsiders, even in the cosmopolitan port city of Casablanca. Her mother came from Western Sahara, to Morocco's south, an unsettled country or region, much in dispute, though under French domination. But being only a quarter-black and pretty, with predominantly Caucasian, minimally black facial features, her daughter often appeared as a light bronze or olive Mediterranean mixture.

A conflicted psyche was further fostered in Dominique who, in addition to being a quarter-black, or three-quarters white, also spoke Arabic as well as French in a country like Morocco, with its Muslim majority population, but mostly a French-speaking officialdom in government. Hoping to find greater opportunity in Paris, where her own artistic ambitions and impulses could be furthered, Dominique became an alter ego for Claudette, whom she met there in a Montmartre art gallery.

At the gallery opening where she first met Dominique, Claudette was initially amazed to see someone so exotic and yet so perfect.

The woman was striking—probably taller than anyone else in the room of either sex—and perfectly proportioned. Moreover, Claudette had never seen anyone with such coloring: smooth, tan, honey-colored skin, carefully coifed black hair, amber eyes—like a cat's. The girl clearly knew how to set off her figure to perfection, wearing a simple sheath in a shade of aquamarine that complemented her complexion.

Claudette found herself marveling at this creature, speculating about where it came from. Her mind strayed to Southern Italy, thence to Greece, finally traveling as far as Syria or elsewhere in the Near East. Central northern Africa was not among the places she considered. As her eyes followed when the girl moved across the room to inspect another painting, Claudette realized that she had never before seen such graceful carriage; and when the girl stood still, Claudette realized that she had already been struck by her elegant natural contrapposto.

At that point the girl turned and gazed directly at Claudette who realized she had been staring most impolitely and quickly turned away.

• • •

Their initial conversation went something like this, after some initial pleasantries.

"Is Casablanca as exotic as I've always heard?" asked Claudette, adding with a slight wistfulness, "I've never had opportunities to travel much anywhere. What's it like? "

"Believe me, you've got things better here in Paris. More openness and contact with people from all over."

"Don't you miss your family?" asked Claudette. "You're still very young to be off on your own like this."

"Well, my father left my mother long ago. He had a rough time in a mixed marriage like theirs, with me as a

27

leftover reminder because of my being quarter-black. Even so, to many my complexion is not mulatto but bronze or olive, not black but light. Anyway, Parisians don't seem to care much one way or the other. They've seen it all."

Claudette didn't press the family comparisons other than to add that her own father had left for America, putting her mother in difficult circumstances.

"After Paris, someday," Dominique went on, "I'd love to travel to America. I hear there's even more artistic–social action in New York City than in Paris."

"If I only knew where to find my father—if he might still be over there."

Dominique then went on to express her surprise at "how little mixed marriages matter in liberal Paris. It's not at all insular, with lots of cross-influences. Nor do Parisians seem to care about Morocco's resistance to French colonization. Paris is a very open city."

When the topic turned to art, including the exhibition they were both attending, the Monet–Picasso contrast in artistic appreciation surfaced soon enough.

"Personally," remarked Dominique, "I really like the newer styles of art nowadays. Like Picasso and the Cubists, or like Matisse and the Fauvists before him. They're all so progressive and avant-garde. It makes me want to try my own hand at this. I also like more straightforward realism. But what about you, Claudette? "

"My own preferences are for Monet, also Renoir. You'll have to come with me sometime to see Monet's villa and gardens. They're so special for visitors as well as his family. Not far from Paris along the Seine."

"I would really enjoy doing that with you. [She hesitates to ask:] Perhaps also someday you'll tell me about your illustrious name and how you're related to the famous Claude Monet."

"It's a long story."

"You would probably have a good welcome in America if you ever went there looking for your father and for new subjects to paint. I hear there are beautiful expansive landscapes and seascapes over there."

"You may well be right, Dominique. I'm sure we could both find good compromise Post-Impressionist models that still carry on Impressionist coloring, form, and 3-D, as well as 2-D."

"Instead of destroying them like the forerunners of Cubism and Abstraction do?" asked Dominique.

"Yes."

4. American Roots

"Tell me more about your American roots," Dominique asked Claudette when they met again at another gallery exhibition in Paris.

"My father came originally from Bucks County, Pennsylvania. He later moved with his mother to Mercer County, New Jersey, after his parents divorced—another conflicted situation. His first and second towns there, Morrisville and Trenton, were on opposite sides of the Delaware River—a very serene and scenic area, I'm told. But I don't want to bore you."

"*Au contraire*," said Dominique, "go on."

"Well, his family farther up river and inland were originally Pennsylvania Quakers who settled there from England in the early eighteenth century."

"Was your father an artist?" asked Dominique. "No, he was a businessman; he met my mother here in Paris when he came on a business trip. But he was interested in the oil paintings being done at that point by Monet and the other Impressionists, because of their beautiful landscapes. He told mother about the American school of Impressionist painters flourishing in and around 'The New Hope Circle' in Bucks County. It's a town not far upstream from Morrisville and just across from Lambertville on the New Jersey side. From there the wide 'Circle' extends upstream in Jersey to Byram and Raven Rock. Mother has told me all this. I've heard and read about this. Now I'm really boring you."

"Have you ever seen any of their works?"

"A few, but not many. I'd like to see more someday. They're still a relatively new school in America, since their formative period; it started around 1900 as a latter-day imitation of Monet's circle of Impressionist painters."

"Have you ever met any of your father's family or relatives?"

"No, but he told mother he had cousins living in the Princeton area of central New Jersey. That's where he went to college and where his father moved after his remarriage. But that was all long ago. Now you're really turned off by all the personal detail for two people who have not been to America."

"Not at all," responded Dominique, "It helps me to understand you better, my dear Claudette."

"It may interest you that two central figures today in French art were both American-born *and* both Pennsylvanians, *and* both from the Pittsburgh area."

"Yes, but who?"

"Mary Cassatt and Gertrude Stein herself."

"But their artistic styles and interests are so far apart," exclaimed Dominique.

"Yes, I know. I suppose you would feel more akin to Gertrude Stein with her connections to Picasso, Cubist art, and the avant-garde."

"Probably, but I also feel more akin to her strong personality as a woman—more dominant, sort of like my own name, 'Dominique'. I suppose you feel closer to Mary Cassatt with softer, more feminine touch as a painter of Impressionist scenes *à la* Monet."

"Of course," replied Claudette. "But Mary Cassatt is a very close associate of Monet, even if she's become a social activist. She's just about his age, whereas Gertrude Stein is a generation younger and far from the Impressionist outlook. Stein and her brothers have collected more progressive painters who are also less expensive than well-established traditionalists like Monet."

• • •

31

As they strolled together along Parisian streets, the massive Eiffel Tower dominated the scene. Claudette joked that France itself probably felt akin to the Tower's spirit of dominance and *erectness*. She remembered vaguely her father once commenting that the French constructed the Eiffel Tower to show the world that France was more than just a loose bunch of fanciful Impressionist painters. She was not sure if he was joking or serious, or both. Certainly that imposing structure *was* an inspiration to the world as well as to the French. "After all," said Claudette, "the tower figures often in impressionist kind of paintings as well as in more modernist ones."

"Agreed," Dominique replied. "So tell me more about your father's roots in the vicinity of 'The New Hope Circle' of Impressionist painters there, up and down both sides of the Delaware River."

"Well, from what mother learned from him, he originally had grandparents and an uncle up the river, back inland from Byram on the New Jersey side. They often invited him to visit their old farmhouse near the top of a hill overlooking the river."

"So I suppose you're partial to that kind of beautiful rural scenery, perfect for Impressionist landscapes all along that whole area."

"Yes. But this is still mostly what my mother remembered from what dad told her. Yet I have seen some picture-books about the American Impressionists."

"Sounds good."

"Not only that, but father's parents shared a summer house along the Jersey shore on Long Beach Island. I vaguely remember how dad used to tell us about that scenic place—another good subject for painting landscapes as well as seascapes."

"So someday you should travel to America to see all that."

They hoped to meet the following Sunday for a stroll along the Seine where they could enjoy the spring sunshine and ogle the fashionable passers-by all dressed in their

Sunday best and looking as though they just stepped out of a Renoir painting.

5. In Search of a Father

Just as they hoped, beautiful weather accompanied their next get-together as they strolled along the banks of the Seine along with plenty of other Parisians, citizens of an Impressionist world all their own.

Dominique asked Claudette how it happened that she knew so much about her lost father's American roots although neither she nor her mother had been able to locate him over all these years.

Claudette's response was involved. An only child, she had been left under the care of an often distracted mother who was preoccupied with her own problems and who had little desire to track down her former husband. Claudette thus felt hobbled in her dreams of ever seeing her American father again. Added to all that was her broken English, like that of her mother (and similar to Dominique's). Eugènie had tried, for her daughter's sake, to write to the last known addresses of Jack Hornsby, even writing to some local authorities in the areas and towns involved, but with no success.

It had all proved to be a daunting task for Eugènie and Claudette. Mostly, everyone indicated that Jack was either missing or deceased. Any known relatives proved unhelpful, providing no solid leads. All that mother and daughter had to go on were the fairly good but sketchy details that the two remembered or had recorded from the time Jack was with them—for the relatively short duration of his courtship and marriage some years earlier. Multiple trans-Atlantic telephone calls and operator informations were still too primitive and expensive a medium. For any hope of resolution, an extended trip to America would be required. And for the time being, such an expedition and search seemed out of the question.

The day ended for the young duo with Claudette more self-confident through her new friend in whom she could confide—but not yet about everything.

• • •

Meanwhile, Claudette was still having dreams about her father. They were long-standing since her early childhood. They started after she and her mother returned home one day to find out that Jack Hornsby had left them for good. For the child it was almost unbearably traumatic. Her mother had no explanation for her. Only later did they learn from passport records that he had gone back to America.

On these dreams and their meaning, Claudette once more confided to Eugènie: "Mother, these dreams about my father still scare me. What can I do about them?"

"I wish I could help comfort you," Eugènie again responded. "What are they about this time?"

"Pretty much the same thing, but they haunt me more after I wake up," came the response.

"Do you want to tell me more?" Eugènie herself was growing more fearful for her daughter's sake. "A few nights ago," began Claudette, "I dreamed that Dominique and I went to America to look for my father. I needed to see if he was still alive and would care about me and help heal this ache in my heart. We went first to New York and then to New Jersey. My name opened some artistic doors for me."

"What then?"

"In central Jersey around the Princeton–Trenton area we were near a river, which I suppose was the Delaware. Suddenly we're walking along a main road past houses set back by their driveways. A mailbox on the roadway in front of one house says 'Hornsby.' I look back a way into the circular driveway, and there's a man standing alone there by a car. He is looking in my direction but without seeming to

35

notice me. So Dominique and I keep walking along the road a few miles into a town."

"That's an OK dream, dear, isn't it?"

"But there's more."

"Go on, dear."

"Last night I had the same dream; but this time the same man was standing there with over a half-dozen others. I go into the driveway all alone to where the people were standing, who have already now gone into the house. I walk over to the house and enter through the door into a vestibule. To the left is the dining room, to the right the living room. I go over into the dining room where they are all sitting at the table. The man sits at the far end facing in my general direction. A woman, probably his wife, sits at the closer, nearer end with her back mostly toward me. Several people sit on each side of the table.

"Then what?" asked her mother.

"No one still seems to notice me. There's an empty side seat on the man's immediate right. I go over and sit down in it, but the man, so close, looks through me. If this is my father, it hurts. One of the other people there is a young girl, six or under, to the man's immediate left, directly across from me. Soon, the dinner, or whatever, is over. The group gets up and, as they are leaving to go to the living room, I actually exchange a few fleeting pleasantries with the woman at the other end. I go outside. Then I wake up in a sweat."

"Why?"

"Come on, mother! Dad has obviously remarried. He has a new wife, whom he loves more than you, and apparently has another daughter more dear to him than I ever was. Worst of all, dad ignores me completely—doesn't care about me or you."

"I see. But don't let it worry you. It's only a dream. We can all have troubling dreams like that. They don't usually mean much, in the end."

"But with all that detail about place and people, do you think I'm somehow clairvoyant?"

36

"Don't worry."

"But I do. Just because your past searches for father through overseas information found no one by his name in that whole area doesn't mean much. And I've had other dreams more disturbing."

"Go on, if you want."

"In one dream," continued Claudette, "I'm on the other side of the Delaware River, near the spot where dad told you is Morrisville. I walk back across the bridge to Trenton in order to attend a Sunday morning church service. It's probably a Protestant service, very different from daddy's Quaker Meetings where people just sit, or stand up to talk if the spirit moves them. All of a sudden, as I'm sitting there listening to the service, a man walks in, goes toward the front platform or altar. He lights up a Camel cigarette. Someone else drags him out and beats him. Daddy is involved, but I'm not sure how."

"Is that all?"

"Not at all. In another dream I'm somewhere again in that vicinity and realize I've not been in touch with daddy there for a long time. I go to an old, half-empty apartment building near the river bridge. I proceed down a narrow empty corridor to the end. I ring the bell, then knock at the door. The door finally opens, and it's Daddy. By now, he's very old and living alone. We both know who the other is. We briefly talk. He is rather passive and concerned that his calcium level is too high from the calcium pills he has been taking. I'm happy to see Daddy, even if the dream ends before either of us can say too much. But at least, he at last connects with me, however briefly. He looked so old and frail, clearly even older than he would look by now. But I have no way of knowing how he would look now after all these years. Would I recognize him? I'm worried about his health and his small living space. I feel bad because I have not seen him for so long and because I can't do anything for him. But if only he is still alive! He didn't seem, in the dream, as if he had much longer to live. What does all this mean, mother?"

37

"Claudette, dear, your wounded inner child is coming out in your dreams. Your dear daddy, I'm sure, would still love you."

"Then why, after all these years, has he never tried to find us? He knows where we are and how to find us, doesn't he?"

"Sort of. Probably."

"One of my other dreams has been about a murder."

"Oh no, honey," giving Claudette a big hug, "but you know how much I love you. God does, too."

"O.K., here it is in a nutshell. Now you tell me if I'm not somehow clairvoyant. People sometimes are, you know. Again, Daddy seems somehow involved along with several others, but I'm not sure how. The dream was over quickly and any details are hazy. Basically, it took place on or near the Delaware River in the area called 'The New Hope Circle,' extending out and up on the Pennsylvania and New Jersey sides. It wasn't clear to me who the victim and killer were, only that they may be connected with daddy and his own circle. He seems to be staying up there somewhere at that point."

"But let's stop for now, dear."

"O.K., but one last thing for now," pressed Claudette, with depth of understanding. "How do I distinguish between reality and fantasy, as if I'm uncertain about a Monet painting that blends the two? The "fantasy sketches" of people and their surroundings in his Impressionist scenes often leave the viewer wondering. Fleeting figures and objects are often left in a shadowy world without clear resolutions. Sort of like me in my waking and sleeping dreams?"

"Someday," replied her mother, "I'm going to have you see a psychologist, if these dreams persist. But it's good to think of Monet. Focus on the bright, happy side of Monet's paintings. Their comforting beauty can help."

"That is true. Thank you, mother."

6. An Aspiring Painter

Meantime, Claudette continued to find refuge from her inner conflicts and heartache in her serene and peaceful world of Impressionist art. Her own fledgling depictions and what she saw in the Paris galleries and exhibitions gave solace.

Claudette also felt the need for new sources of scenic inspiration as well as potential new buyers for her creations. She had heard about the thriving New York City market for Impressionist painting, still popular in her day into the early 1920s. Her name might yet bear the fruit her mother envisioned for her when she changed their name from Hornsby to Monet.

By now Claudette's modest part-time day job (working for a Parisian art-supply company) was moving along well. She was earning enough to make it worthwhile, even if not sufficient for a trip to America. There, she hoped, her artistic and personal contacts might lead to promising opportunities.

At her job, Claudette also met an older man, Jacques Moreau. He supplied the store with some art supplies such as an inexpensive type of canvas that appealed to poorer painters, as well as stretchers that were equally cheap but inclined to spear their users with splinters while being assembled. There were also a good-quality imported gouache made in England, and a number of other items. Since one of Claudette's duties as the store's most menial employee was checking the inventory of everything they stocked, she found herself spending time with Jacques, whom she found herself liking.

He was twelve years older than Claudette, tall and saturnine, with thinning hair and a luxuriant graying moustache. She began to compare him with her receding memories of her father. When he asked her to dinner, she was only too willing to accept, and thought herself lavishly entertained to be taken to bistros only a cut or two above those she patronized with her mother. Because Jacques had served his country with distinction in the late war and wore the *Croix de Guerre*, he was treated with deference everywhere they went. Better still to Claudette, here was an older man who asked her opinions about art and listened attentively to her replies. He also showered her with painting supplies, gifts from the better lines he carried.

Then he began to escort her to openings at galleries where he was connected, sometimes including Dominique in their party and dining afterward. When Claudette and Dominique began fantasizing about their trip to America, he told them to follow their dream.

Seduced by all this attention, Claudette soon found herself seduced in the more traditional sense. She acquiesced to Jacques's advances more out of a sense of obligation than for any great love she bore him, but she did not find his lovemaking distasteful either. Seeing how well he lived with a much larger apartment than she and her mother could afford, as well as a cleaning lady to keep it tidy and a large room she could use as a studio—she felt she could not refuse the proposal of marriage that came along soon.

Her one stipulation, made very specifically to the bridegroom before she accepted his proposal, was that there would be no children, not for a while anyway.

• • •

It was Jacques who supplied better *entrée* for Claudette into two key venues of the Parisian art world. The first was the Giverny estate of Claude Monet with its spacious gardens. Through this fuller, more direct access, they duly inspired her as they had many other artists. The

Impressionist legacy would always be alive at Giverny, even if somewhat faded by the time of Monet's death in 1926. By then, Claudette in fact would be in America. There, that legacy would long remain vibrant. By the time Claudette became more familiar with Claude Monet's Giverny, his visual impairments had rendered him somewhat reclusive. His complicated life there involved extended circles of family and friends having their own various marital name changes. Any possible embarrassment or awkwardness over Claudette's own name change was largely taken away. Before that time, Claude himself had often been preoccupied elsewhere in Western Europe at a time when she was too young or inexperienced for such things to matter much. Anyway, the name change was by then mostly a non-issue. Yet it could still be perceived as an asset as well as a pose in the usually liberal wider French art world.

"What a thrill it was for both Dominique and me to explore Giverny and Monet's world there," Claudette told her mother. "I was maybe too young to appreciate it enough when you and I went there years ago. This time we were able to meet and talk briefly with a few of the people staying there. They seemed interested and encouraging."

"I'm so happy for you and your friend, dear."

"Yes," Claudette continued. "Now I get a better sense of how Claude Monet and many others used those extensive beautiful gardens and nearby natural settings in their paintings. But one can also see how they turned actual scenes into creations quite unlike those original models. That's what I'd like to do in a landscape world of new possibilities especially in America."

The second venue that Jacques Moreau helped supply for Claudette was the art collection and circle of Gertrude Stein and Alice B. Toklas, another legendary focal point for artists of all kinds in that era. Stein's collection at her home on the Rue de Fleurus included all sorts of paintings. There Gertrude gave encouragement to artists great and small. She favored (less expensive) avant-garde rather than more traditional (and costly) impressionist painters. The same had

41

been true for brother, Leo, before their split in 1913. Gertrude's noted acquisitions of Picasso's art came early on for both patron and artist, especially prior to World War I before added stature came to them. Cubism was, then, by no means the only one of Picasso's many evolving styles she collected. Stein's interests ranged far and wide, beyond a single artistic expression. Thus Claudette was duly awed when she attended some of Stein's noted salon gatherings in the early 1920s. She knew that these more avant-garde styles were also thriving in the American art markets, chiefly in New York City; but she still kept her favored Impressionist preferences.

• • •

"I went with Jacques yesterday to see the famous Stein collection, and it's awesome," Claudette excitedly told Dominique when they met one day for lunch.

"I haven't been there yet, but I hope to do so," her friend answered. "Did you see Gertrude Stein herself?"

"Yes, briefly. That's why I went with Jacques, who has made her acquaintance in the past through his art supply business. She took an interest in my aspirations and wished me well. In the male-dominated art world, she's unusual. But it's encouraging to find someone with her stature who takes an interest in would-be female painters."

Replied Dominique, "I'd find her interesting, too. I hear she's masculine-looking, sometimes having close personal involvements with other women, even though Alice Toklas remains her partner."

"I've heard all that before from mother, too. When I was much younger, she secured an invitation and took me briefly to see the Stein collections. That was before Gertrude and Leo split up in 1913. But I don't recall much from that visit. There are so many paintings there today all over the walls looks like the old official state-sponsored salon exhibits, not like just another art gallery."

"What impressed you most now, Claudette?"

"Perhaps the earlier paintings by Modernists like Matisse and Picasso. They're so numerous and striking. You would especially like them, too. It's said that they and those by other important painters were bought by the Steins at very low prices, fresh through dealers from the artists themselves, before and into the war years."

"Did Gertrude Stein take note of your name? Did she ask if and how you're related to Claude Monet?"

"Yes, but only in passing. Again, my encounter with her was brief. 'Actually,' I said to her, 'I'm only related indirectly through a distant cousin. It's a long story.' So we left it at that. That's pretty much what I've also told you. Jacques says I should no longer feel conflicted over mother's name change for me. I'm pretty comfortable with it by now, even if I often feel guilty for not bearing my father's name. I'm still the daughter of Jack Hornsby."

"And your mother?"

"Mother felt it was too unpromising a name for her as well as for me in the French artistic–social world, where image can count for something. She would rhetorically ask out loud, 'Clarissa Hornsby?' to justify her early name changes and frictions with daddy."

"I think you're beautiful just the way you are, Claudette."

"Thank you, Dominique."

"*Please* call me Monique. As I've said, it's what my close family and friends called me."

"O.K., Monique. Now if I can only get Jacques to help arrange for mother an invitation to some of Gertrude Stein's bigger, more formal Saturday night salon get-togethers. Then she could really meet people and see all the paintings by others like Cezanne, Renoir, and Pissarro."

Said Monique, "I'd love to meet Gertrude, too, and talk about all the writing she's done besides the art she's collected and sometimes sold."

"Jacques says that her family's wealth, although not as great as some say, was amassed in the United States, especially California. It became a real springboard for her.

What an artistic–social world it has opened up for her, with lots of cross-contacts between France and America. Maybe I could find openings there to go from Paris to New York."

• • •

To be sure, Gertrude Stein became a cultural icon for so many.

In 1906, Pablo Picasso painted a portrait of Gertrude Stein sitting with her arms resting on her thighs and scowling like a hanging judge. Someone commented that Stein didn't look like that. "She will," Picasso replied. And indeed she did. The photographs Carl Van Vechten took of her in the 1930s look very much like Picasso's Portrait.

She was short and squat with a tendency to overweight that she fought all her life (not helped by the food Alice B. Toklas, her lover, prepared so assiduously), but she carried herself like an empress. And her manner, coupled with her absolute assertion of authority on all subjects, made her indeed formidable. Behind her back, members of her circle called her "Le Stein" or less reverently, "The Presence." For many years she was largely famous for being famous: Gertrude Stein who wrote incomprehensible poetry. If the man in the street knew anything about her, it would be lines like "Pigeons on the grass, alas" or "A rose is a rose is a rose." Not until 1933, when she wrote *The Autobiography of Alice B. Toklas* (all about the greatness of Gertrude Stein) did she become a significant literary presence.

From 1904 to 1914, she and her brother Leo shared a house in Paris, where Leo maintained a studio. They systematically tapped into their trust fund to support their taste for modern art. Thanks largely to Leo's discernment, they acquired some of the greatest works of the masters of the day: Cézanne, Gauguin, Renoir, Delacroix, Toulouse-Lautrec, and, of course, Matisse and Picasso. Their collection became so well known that they held a salon every Saturday evening where their friends and hangers-on were welcome to talk and admire the art.

44

Something happened in 1914 besides the outbreak of the Great War. Gertrude and Leo had a falling out, a rupture so acrimonious that they never spoke to one another again, or rarely so. Leo packed up his share of the collection (the Renoirs and other more establishment paintings) and took them with him to Florence. The Saturday salons came to an end. Gertrude kept the more avant-garde painters; but lacking Leo's discernment and with an increasing involvement in matters literary, as well as a shrinking trust fund, she collected less and less and tended to select second-rank artists. Ultimately, she sold many of her most valuable items to finance publication of her books or simply to put food on her table. Her involvement with the visual arts in the period between the wars was lower.

Although, she worked very hard at her own writing, she also found time to dispense advice to squadrons of American expatriates like Hemingway, Wilder, and others less gifted.

7. Echoes from the Jazz Age

By the early 1920s, then, after the War, Claudette occasionally attended a Stein salon and visited the Monet Gardens. Both venues were changing. Gertrude Stein and her brother, Leo, already split apart, along with other family members, were dividing up further pieces of their art collections. Gertrude was more intent on her writing. Meanwhile, Claude Monet was suffering from physical ailments and becoming a reclusive figure, gathering family members and friends around him.

Nevertheless, both of these places and personalities were still exerting great influences.

The Stein collection and salons had become extensively international in scope. A widening array of artists, writers, and socialites was on display there in a fashionable setting near the Luxembourg Gardens and River Seine. To visit the Stein apartments housing the art collection and hosting the salons usually required knowing someone and feeling up to par around the Steins and their circle. Guests from all over could be encountered there. Particularly in evidence were visitors from New York City, where the Jazz Age and its accompaniments in art and literature were already in full swing. New Yorkers in Paris and Parisians in New York were becoming vibrant interchanges; they worked their spell on the impressionable, young Claudette, enticing her all the more to venture overseas. Paris was attracting noted American writers like Fitzgerald, as was London with others like T.S. Eliot, along with influxes of travelers. All were helping to revive spirits and culture after the devastating war years.

At the same time, not far downriver from Paris, many visitors were drawn to the Monet Gardens and their surroundings. Impressionism was still in vogue, even in faraway places like the American northeast. New York visitors to Giverny were leaving their own impressions as well as taking others home with them. It was not lost on these travelers that the Stein collections of Leo, before he took many to Italy earlier on, included works by Renoir, Pissarro, and Cézanne. These were more traditional and related to Impressionism. Gertrude's preferences ran more to progressive painters like Picasso, Braque, and Matisse. Perhaps the Stein collection would have included Monet if his works had not by then become so expensive and well established in popular sentiment.

• • •

"I find it again interesting," Claudette told her husband, "that two women from America, both from the same area in Pennsylvania, are having such influence here around Paris. Mary Cassatt has been key for Impressionism and Gertrude Stein for more avant-garde artists like Picasso. I see that painters in artistic centers like New York are creating their own different styles relating to both varieties. I've seen some of their exhibition catalogues; but I'd love to visit there to see better for myself."

"Yes, dear, you should go to New York someday. But not yet—I still need you here and I'm still not free to travel much because of my business. Anyway, I don't want you going over there all alone, yet."

"Could I go with Dominique?"

"I'd rather you don't."

"Why not? People at both the Stein and Monet places have encouraged me to go. It's so exciting in America. The swing music by the jazz bands is really catching on."

"No! I need you here!"

But by now a trip to New York City, their first big stop, was gaining an almost irresistible momentum for Claudette and Dominique. "Think of all the excitement over there," said Dominique.

She was really reinforcing and pressing Claudette as she continued talking to her. "Just think about all the stories we've been hearing from Americans here in Paris about New York in the Jazz Age—the Harlem Renaissance and the Roaring Twenties. And all the new music, art, and literature in vogue over there. A thriving international art market. All the avant-garde progressive and traditional European art being held in such high esteem over there."

"What else?"

"Think of all the night life in Greenwich Village and the bustling street scenes there in the daytime. Don't forget bootleggers, Prohibition, and speakeasies. The Charleston dance craze. The chance to meet lots of new people. A booming stock market producing lots of new money for parties and projects."

"Let the good times roll, and let's roll with them?" asked Claudette.

"Yes, that's the spirit," retorted Dominique. "But what about Jacques' refusal to let me go, even with you as a companion? He does control the purse strings, you know, despite my modest part-time job."

Countered Dominique: "We can 'swing it,' like the Big Bands over there. Let's save up enough for the ocean passage to New York and then get part-time jobs once we get there. Maybe I'll even find a handsome husband of my own to help us. Anyway, your illustrious name will help give us *entrée* over there."

"But what to do about Jacques? There are so many levels to all this. But as you say—new scenes to paint, new people to meet, new markets for art, new dances to learn, new chances to resolve old problems, including the whereabouts of my father."

• • •

If the "roaring twenties," epitomized by the Charleston, were now taking off faster in America, they would eventually roar in France too, once the greater wartime traumas there subsided. But in the early years of the decade America already held out special Jazz Age attractions for the two young women.

8. Leaving Husband Behind

Claudette was right; there were conflicts between many levels of a complex personality (not only his but hers) in her efforts to leave Jacques behind and depart with Dominique for New York. An unexpectedly shadowy Jacques was bringing out the need for new resolve in Claudette.

"For one thing," she confided to her mother, "there is the question of how to do this. I'll just have to leave without saying goodbye, for fear of a jealous rage from him. He has become so possessive, even obsessive. He never used to be like that. I'll have to leave him a note saying I'll only be gone a few months and will write often."

"Shades of how your father left you and me so abruptly, dear? Sounds like the old saying about the sins of the parents being visited upon their children?"

"I suppose you're right, mother."

"But you know, I'll support your decision to go and pursue your dreams. I'll give you what little money I can afford to help get you started."

"I do see Jacques as a father figure I've feared and respected as well as loved. When I call him by his name, I sometimes think of Daddy's American equivalent, Jack."

"Is this your inner way of telling your father know how hurt you still are by his walking out on you without a goodbye?"

"You may be right, but what else can I do? Jacques wouldn't follow me, would he?"

"Try not to worry about that," Eugènie replied. "By the way, changing the topic, how are you and Dominique getting along in the midst of all this? I hope that by now you'll both be comfortable spending so much new time with each other? "

"Of course, mother. She sometimes reminds me, as her good friend, to call her Monique."

"How do you think people in America will react to Monique being a quarter black, a mulatto, and to you two acting as a couple? Or to each of you speaking broken English? As you say, most people over here don't think her light bronze or olive color is Negroid—or even care. But over there, would they question things like that?"

"I don't see why there would be a problem, do you? Why do you ask about people's reaction to us as a couple? Are you getting at something?"

"Claudette, dear, you know that as a parent I've had some so-called sins of my own here in our country that I'm not sure I would want to pass on to you. I just don't want to see you so close to your friend, far from home on another continent, with things getting out of hand."

"Mother! Why do you say that? Monique and I have never discussed sex like that. A few times she's come up with the unheard-of term 'metrosexual' for some people, but nothing more even about that, whatever it means."

"I hope there's no racial prejudice over there to get in your way," continued Eugènie. "Paris is pretty open and cosmopolitan about such things as race and sex. I hope the same is true of New York City, but other places inland may be less accepting or tolerant of foreigners, blacks, and same-sex involvements. Just be careful and stay in touch with me—and with your husband."

"Of course, mother. I love you so much for all you've tried to do. Don't worry."

"After you've gone, I'll try to smooth things over with Jacques and assure him you'll keep in touch and not be gone long."

"Thank you so much."

• • •

51

Later, as they prepared to embark, Dominique doubtless had her own meditations with other friends on the adventures lying ahead or already at hand. "In a sense," she might have soliloquized, "I'm more vulnerable and alone than Claudette. She at least has a mother and husband here in France. She has or had a father with a background in America. I, on the other hand, have already felt alone here in my adopted country. My family in Morocco has been dispersed, and I've had little contact with my mother. Claudette and her family have become my only real family or sense of belonging here in Paris. So I'm really going to depend on her to be my mainstay in America. Claudette already has a better sense than I do about the places she wants us to visit. I feel so attached to her. We seem so right for each other. Now I'll get to be even closer. I hope this all turns out right. I was already used to the adventure of leaving Casablanca for Paris; but it's all even greater now—leaving Paris for New York. Claudette at least already has a purpose for doing this, pursuing her painting and her father. I'm not yet so sure about myself. But we'll both be depending on each other."

For now, the excitement of new adventure filled their horizon.

Part Two: America

9. New York Scenes

Even more so than Paris, New York City in the mid-1920s was surging forth with post-war energies. As new arrivals, Claudette and Dominique (or Monique as Claudette usually called her) found it all overwhelming but exciting. Arriving in New York Harbor, Claudette was already imagining new scenes to paint whether in Impressionist or Realist styles. Being more dominant (as befitted her name), Dominique was more concerned at that point about arranging for a place to stay. They had made no prior arrangements for lodging, trusting that things would unfold suitably once they arrived and had a sense of their surroundings.

After their first night in a small hotel near Washington Square Park in Greenwich Village, the newly-arrived pair went to an Artists' League office, which the hotel manager told them about. The league had connections with nearby New York University and seemed full of other potential contacts for them. There, they befriended an older professor who was happy to show them around and to help them become more settled in the area. Soon they strolled through the park near the big Washington Arch at the bottom of Fifth Avenue. They talked with several outdoor painters who were taking advantage of the sunny spring day as in *Paris en plein air* with palette in hand for mixing colors.

They seemed off to a good start.

Fortunately, Dominique's darker but uncertain skin color was not perceived, in that segregated era, as a bar to housing or employment. Through such encounters, opportunities opened up for more suitable lodging and possibilities for employment. Perhaps because of her exotic appearance (something unexpected and French but hardly African) Dominique's appearance did not trigger any protests—notwithstanding strict segregation amid the city's cosmopolitanism. She and Claudette went wherever they chose, with whomever they met in New York and nobody tried to stop them.

•••

As it soon turned out, the professor was himself a fledgling painter in oil and watercolor during his spare time as a popular outgoing figure around the campus. He seemed as interested in someday visiting the Parisian orbits around Monet and Stein as the two women were in coming to New York. Clearly the name Claudette Monet was "an ace in the hole" for the pair. They all had much to talk about. The two women were only too happy to take him up on his offer to show them around the city. He was obviously taking a personal interest in them, Claudette in particular. His name, John Haverstraw, resonated for Claudette with surprising similarity to those of her father, Jack, and her husband, Jacques. Was an older man again going to vie with Dominique, however subtly, for Claudette's attention?

It would become the makings of another complex relationship for Claudette. But who, further, was he?

John Haverstraw (he often preferred Jack to John, Claudette soon learned) was a leading professor at NYU of the relatively new field of sociology, which attempted to quantify the behavior of people in societies. Being a skilled observer and a man of generous nature, John had long since concluded that the inferiority of black Americans was largely an expression of white Americans' need to feel superior. Armed with this knowledge, he had formed many deep and lasting friendships with black people. With the Harlem Renaissance in full swing, Harlem had become a hotbed of literary and artistic activity, and Jack loved being in the middle of it all.

John, or Jack, was born and bred in the Berkshire Hills of western Massachusetts, son of a merchant family. He even took his degree at Williams College. By then he had attained his full height of six feet, four inches and his fighting weight of 160 pounds. Noticing that tall people tend to develop a permanent stoop, he promised himself always to stand up straight (hearing his mother's voice every time he thought of this: "Stand up straight, Jack, or you'll turn into a hunchback." "If I stand up straight, Mother, I'll hit the chandelier with my head.")

He tried to undercut the impression of imperiousness conveyed by his height by cultivating an attitude of extreme affability. Hence, he introduced himself as Jack and told anyone who asked that he was a teacher (never a professor). Already at the apex of his career and despite the graying hair, he was only thirty-four years old; it gave him a bit of a frisson to hear Claudette refer to him as "an older man," who reminded her of her husband (who was an ancient thirty-six). At one point, Jack thought of growing a beard, but decided against it because he thought it would make him look too much like Thorstein Veblen.

With money from his family, Jack Haverstraw had bought a rangy old house on St. Luke's Place, and he delighted in offending his snobbish neighbors by inviting a varied mixture of races to his parties. These affairs usually took place on Monday nights, when even the nightclubs of Harlem were pretty dreary. When he invited Duke Ellington or Count Basie, he always made it clear that they were under no obligation to play, just to enjoy themselves. Inevitably they'd take one look at Jack's seven-foot Steinway and (with the memories of all the terrible instruments they'd faced over the years clanging in their ears) yielded to its temptation, to the delight of everyone there.

• • •

Claudette was soon writing to her mother in Paris about some of the New York scenes she and Dominique were 'taking in'. "Our new American friend, John Haverstraw, has been introducing us to some of his friends, including a few who are black or mixed race. A group of us went uptown last weekend to where the Harlem Renaissance is in full swing. The 'Roaring Twenties' are really roaring up there. Monique and I both love all the excitement at the many speakeasies, often owned by bootleggers and sometimes open to anyone. People call this the Jazz Age because of the wild, swinging music everyone is dancing to until late at night. You'd never guess that this is also the Prohibition Era, outlawing drinking. People up there and everywhere are drinking more than ever. With our friend John's contacts, we are getting into lots of clubs. Black musicians do all the playing, with loud sounds from their trombones, clarinets, bass fiddles, and so forth. But at more formal places like the Cotton Club, black people as patrons doing the dancing are not seen.

"So," she went on, "we often avoid them because of John's black friends who come with us and Monique's potential problem. John knows about Dominique being a quarter-black; but he agrees that her light bronze or olive color is generally OK and shouldn't give her away, especially at night. But we have to be even more careful whenever we go with John's black friends.

"Racial prejudice," Claudette continued, "still runs deep in America, much more so than in France, even in a cosmopolitan city like New York, though not as deeply as in the American South. Segregated housing is still the norm, but we're OK so far. If questions arise, we turn them aside. Women dancing with women, if they entered without a male partner are also not seen much— again a less liberal attitude here than in Paris. Monique and I have sometimes danced together in Paris, no problem; but over here, even in New York, people tend to frown and either look away or stare. I wonder how much more prejudiced people still are outside centers like New York. We hear that in the South there are still racial lynchings for small infractions against racial taboos. But Monique seems unfazed, which is good. The black musicians here seem unfazed, too. With players like

Count Basie and Louis Armstrong, how can we miss? Mother, you should see what the women are wearing to such places! But that's another story for another day."

• • •

Writing to her husband back in Paris, Claudette was naturally careful not to tell him about her adventurous night life in New York; rather, she wrote about her impressions of New York scenes lending themselves to painting. After all, that was her stated purpose for going, aside from finding her father. Jacques' responses were leaving mixed questions in her mind. Was he coming around to an acceptance of her promised short stay in America? Or would he still turn his penchant for anger into wrath and vengeance? To date, he had sent Claudette no money to help her, and her mother's ability to do so had reached its limits. The part-time jobs in art supply firms were agreeable but tight for Claudette and Dominique, though they were now living in more suitable but temporary circumstances. So far, she reported to Jacques, Dominique's usually ambiguous coloring had generally not raised suspicions or presented racial problems in their housing or employment.

"You would love it here in New York, Jacques," Claudette wrote. "So many new sights to explore: active street scenes in Greenwich Village around Washington Square Park. Boating scenes in Central Park with Sunday strollers. Ferryboat rides along the Hudson and East Rivers. Beach and sea-scape scenes along the Coney Island boardwalk. Landscape scenes around Staten Island and Governor's Island, where there's a thriving art colony looking across the bay to the lower Manhattan skyline. I see the need to adapt Impressionist viewpoints to these other conditions, and to mix them with more Realist or Naturalist techniques. Time will tell. The art market here for Impressionist paintings is thriving, including a fondness for our French masters like Monet. It is true that such new crazes as Art Deco have led to some new contemporary

59

forms more in keeping with the tempo of the 'Roaring Twenties.' They are perceived by some critics as a rebellion against more placid Impressionist modes. If you ever want to get involved directly with the New York art market and its opportunities for selling your art supplies, this is fertile ground. Our art supply jobs here give us good glimpses into all that. Also, access to art supplies for our own works, which we hope to sell. There are lots of chances for us to see paintings of all kinds in the galleries and exhibitions. Especially rewarding are the rich collections of paintings, both traditional and contemporary, in the Metropolitan Museum of Art with lots of Monets and other Impressionist works."

But Claudette's letters to her mother continued to paint much different scenes of the active social life she and Dominique were experiencing. Claudette was engaging or indulging in an active nightlife centered around an admiring John Haverstraw and his friends. Dominique was beginning to feel left out, her nose feeling somewhat out of joint. Claudette was now dating other men, with some intimate involvements that often left her distracted.

• • •

After a while, Claudette was becoming less attuned to, because she was less affected by it, the continued partial backlash against blacks and foreigners in the aftermath of the war. Outside of Harlem, a young quarter-black woman from Morocco who spoke broken English could still encounter prejudice, depending on the case, even more so outside other big northern cities in the country sides. The poetry, at that time, of the black writer, Langston Hughes, told the plight still facing blacks as outsiders, even in New York City. Dominique was struck by this theme as she grappled with Hughes's poems. A new better sense of black identity was slowly emerging then, but it had a long way to go amid setbacks. Fortunately, Dominique was seldom perceived as mulatto, but it sometimes weighed on her. Segregation was still widespread.

"Mother, please don't let on," wrote Claudette, "if and when you speak to Jacques, about my active social nightlife here in New York. I don't know what he might try to do. It's bad enough if Dominique starts to feel left out. But I don't want to get Jacques' jealous rage fired up against me. I go with John and sometimes other men to the speakeasies, the strip joints, the jazz bands, the movies, the restaurants, the art shows and exhibits, the sports games, and more. All this in less than a year of being over here. We try not to drink too much Jack Daniels (still another Jack?) at places like Happy Roanes, so we don't start our jobs with a hangover in the mornings."

"Through it all," she said, "we usually still try to be careful not to be seen socializing much with blacks in the daytime, to avoid problems; but at night we manage to hit those spots more favorable to racial mixing. Dominique's neutral darker color usually avoids suspicion, but she sometimes gets self-conscious. She and I both miss the openness of Paris. We wonder what the rest of America is like."

10. "Feminists" and Flappers

John Haverstraw's extended circle of friends in New York's Greenwich Village was having its influence on the two impressionable women from Paris. "You're both looking more and more like typical pretty females in our Jazz Age." "I hope so," replied Claudette, "it suits us well."

Dominique was nevertheless slower to adapt than was Claudette.

"You must realize," Haverstraw continued, "that the ideal symbol today for women of the Jazz Age is called The Flapper. Her role is a rebellion against the Victorian Age. Back then, women wore long hair, long dresses, long faces, less makeup, less perfume, and less colorful styles. Today all that has changed."

"Why?" asked Dominique.

Ever the teacher, despite his flair for the good times at hand, John started to explain. "In part, the suffragette movement, which finally won women the vote in 1920, eventually opened up new doors for American women. Social and cultural changes soon followed, more quickly than in Europe. There, Victorianism often lingered longer despite innovations."

Sounding for a moment like one of John's students, Claudette was quick with a question, "What do you mean by feminism? It's not a term I'm familiar with."

The conversation shifted abruptly as one of John's lady friends entered the room. She was flamboyant in her evening attire. More so than those in John's regular circle as they gathered at his place to go together up to those Harlem night spots accessible to black patrons along 125 Street and above.

"Rebecca, dear," said John, "Claudette and Dominique are here from France. They've been asking me about Victorianism, flappers, and feminism."

Rebecca was all ears: "Let's hear it."

"Well, for instance," he continued for the gathering group, "notice Rebecca's short bobbed hair, her short bright dress, her white hose turned down at her powdered knees, and her thick make-up, long flashy necklace, and stylish shoes."

As Rebecca's dance partner for the evening was then entering, Claudette again asked John, "So what do you mean by feminism?"

At that point, Rebecca's dance partner, half-black and darker—was busy looking at Dominique, who seemed not to notice, observing Rebecca instead. Dominique was awaiting the blind date whom John, Claudette's date, had arranged for her. "Feminism in our day," began John, "can mean many different things. It is a fairly new term I and others use for post-suffragette advances by today's feminine movement. It means more freedom for women in public as well as in private life. More and more women now feel free to smoke and drink in public, to put on their makeup in public, and to dress more freely at work as they have been doing privately or in the nightclubs. With their right to vote, they have been entering more into the social and political mainstream with men. Women's rights have been an influence at home and in marriage. Wives are no longer as subservient as they once were in the Victorian Age. For another thing, women's rights have been slowly leading to a sense of women's power in helping to shape public policy. All this remains for future feminists to fulfill in their own way."

"They still have a long way to go," remarked Dominique.

"Tell all this to my husband," declared Claudette. "He clings still to the old-fashioned idea of women as subservient to their husbands. Jacques was strongly against my coming to America alone or with Dominique, so I had to sneak off. I

63

still fear he may yet come here after me. He is a very jealous person, and angry when he can't control me."

• • •

At the nightspots where the group went, the Charleston, the Black Bottom, and the Lindy (Jitterbug) were the dance crazes as the Jazz bands loudly performed. Spirits were high. Claudette typically glimpsed possible scenes as subjects for painting. "It strikes me, John, that the black musicians are all male, not a single woman."

"I know," he answered, "and the people dancing are all white except for Dominique and her date. Yet she is not seen as black and her date is OK in the dimly-lit clubs we're going to. Dominique still doesn't seem too comfortable in her toned-down party clothes, unlike Rebecca or even you. Yet Dominique seems to admire Rebecca's stylish attire, even dancing with her to get a better sense of the dance steps. But I imagine a black woman would feel a little odd in full flapper garb amid a generally whites-only clientele."

Added Claudette, "I have been trying to loosen her up so that she feels more comfortable on the dance floor. She's getting the hang of things, better than at first."

"She obviously adores you, Claudette—even to the point of loving you. I hope she's not a jealous type like your estranged husband. I wouldn't want them both coming after me, the way you fear Jacques will come after you."

"Don't worry," said Claudette.

Periodically, the band leader would shout out, "Heidi, Heidi, Hi," and the dancers would call back the familiar response of "Heidi, Heidi, Ho." The horns blared, the drums beat, and the booze flowed. Claudette put it well to Dominique when she reassuringly said, "Our bistros and cabarets in Paris were never quite like these clubs, were they? If I were Renoir, I would find these scenes a little too wild for my paintings."

"I know what you mean. Here even the smaller speakeasies are a little too free and easy."

Conversation was drowned out.

• • •

Jazz band, Jazz band, play, play, play,
Still going strong into the night.
The horns are blaring,
The drums beat forth,
The booze keeps flowing.
Dance, dance, dance the night away.
Come join in.
Heidi, Heidi, Hi,
Heidi, Heidi, Ho.
Other bands take over,
Long into the night.
Hi, Hi, Hi, Ho, Ho, Ho.

11. Death of the Master

Time passed more swiftly than the two women realized...
When news came to Claudette, through the public press
in 1926, that the cherished Claude Monet had died, she
quickly wrote to her mother. "What might this mean for his
ongoing legacy and appeal?"

Eugènie wrote back, "Monet will enjoy a perennial
appeal for French and Americans alike. So, too, will
Impressionism more generally along with the disparate
varieties of Post-Impressionism."

Eugènie was right. For a time, the Master's demise
brought renewed public interest in him, in his art, and in his
legendary life at Giverny and elsewhere. Even the name
Claudette Monet brought renewed recognition for her.

"Too bad he never went to America. Then you'd have an
even better shot at name-recognition," commented Eugènie,
ever the ambitious calculator.

Even among art critics and dealers, to be sure, the Monet
name never really lost its stature in America or in France.

As the Roaring Twenties were opening more doors for
women, Eugènie continued to hope that her daughter's name
would help doors to open up even more, especially in the art
world. Eugènie even hoped that a renewed American interest
in Paris would rub off a little on Parisians like her daughter
living in New York. American post-war isolationism was
fading. A new internationalism was growing. These trends
would soon be furthered by Lindbergh's flight in 1927 and
Gershwin's composition *An American in Paris* in 1928.

"Unfortunately," Claudette wrote to Eugènie, "I've
gotten a little sidetracked here in New York City. Between

the nightlife and my art supply job, I haven't been able to devote much time and energy to the painting I hoped to do here. I also haven't been able to search for my father as I intended to do. So I really need to leave the city and go on to New Jersey and Pennsylvania to find good landscape scenery and pursue leads on Daddy's whereabouts. Dominique has been a big help and friend. She's likewise looking forward to those adventures. We keep coming back to our original question—'If Monet had come to America, what would he have painted and how?'"

In one of her letters to Claudette after Claude Monet's death, Eugènie passed along troubling news. "Your husband Jacques worries me. I'm not sure what he intends to do. Recently he expressed angry feelings, still, about your sudden departure and long absence. He even made veiled threats about going to New York to take you back with him. To me, it sounded like a jealous rage. Through the art supply business, he seems to have picked up news about your active nightlife, including your association with other men like John Haverstraw. I'm not sure what to say or do, if anything, at this point with him. Would Jacques—or even your friend, John—ever try to expose your close relationship with a mulatto woman?"

• • •

Although this news alarmed Claudette and Dominique, they were at first unsure how to react or what to do. Their alarm and indecision were a painful mixture that strangely brought them closer together. For some time their paths and interests had been diverging. Even while inhabiting the same apartment and social world, they had been slowly growing apart.

Once they decided on the best course of action, they felt closer to each other. Their plan now entailed going alone together down across New Jersey and into Pennsylvania, and even beyond. In order to accomplish this, they needed the cooperation of their by-now good friend and ally, John

Haverstraw. He would guard against any informers in the art supply business from finding out about the pair's whereabouts. John readily agreed to this and wished them well. Yet, he did so with mixed emotions due to his growing affections for Claudette, with whom he apparently had sporadic sexual relations. John was also urged to watch out for the unnamed man who had occasionally accompanied Rebecca on their evening escapades the one who had warily eyed Dominique. There seemed to remain a big question mark about him.

Making matters even more complicated were again issues over race and sex, pressing the pair all the more to depart from New York. In another hasty letter to her mother, Claudette conceded she and Dominique had become careless. By associating too closely with John Haverstraw, and ignoring his known association with blacks, people like Rebecca's darker, more obviously mulatto friend were bringing adverse attention. Dominique's less obvious mulatto coloring was being given away, breaking many taboos of those days in the process.

Claudette wrote: "We are starting to be denied entrance to certain Harlem nightclubs that previously gave us no trouble. Threats have been made against us. We've been accused of living together as a mixed-race lesbian couple, who come as immigrants from a foreign country and speak broken English. France and Paris are so liberal by comparison. People are said to be even less tolerant outside New York."

Referring to news about the death of Claude Monet, Claudette continued: "We have tried all along to remind people about his importance. We were painting even more in full public view, open-air, around lower Manhattan near where we live and work. We hoped to get more people interested enough to buy our artwork. But in the bright, warm sunlight Dominique's more exposed body drew attention to her color not just light Mediterranean bronze or olive, but a more clearly mulatto mixture. It was the wrong kind of publicity. Outside New York, we're thinking of saying Dominique is my traveling maid. That way, we avoid suspicions in the wrong places for unsegregated mixed associations like ours. The problem with this is that some people may not believe us because it will be obvious that I can't afford a full-time maid. We fear someone coming after us as a mixed lesbian couple. At least things aren't as bad here as in the American South. There, black men can be lynched just for whistling at a white woman. It has taken us a while to catch on about some troubling social issues in these times.

12. Intimate Involvements

What else was now transpiring between the two women?

In the busy new social worlds or whirls of Paris and New York, Claudette and Dominique had not been accustomed to being, just the two of them, alone together. Their "tale of two cities" had involved active, even crowded, surroundings of city people in a major metropolitan area. Now they were going alone together into an unknown hinterland, where their colors and foreign accents would stand out more vividly. It was a daunting yet promising adventure. They looked to each other for mutual reassurance and security.

Claudette had already read quite a lot about the parts of New Jersey and Pennsylvania where her father had had close connections and where she might find good prospects for *plein air* landscape painting. Actually, in her mind, just finding those places and people without a guide would be a challenge. The whole experience of setting out to do what she had for so long been preparing for made her feel frighteningly vulnerable, and she needed her partner's understanding presence to help and steady her.

There was lots of hugging and more. Dominique had long been the more dominant, even possessive of the two. Claudette was more yielding and submissive when it came to their social life and travel plans together. Although it was basically Claudette's personal star they were following, Claudette somehow found Dominique's stature imposing. Dominique, in turn, found Claudette's more youthful, gentle charm appealing. Each seemed to bring out her partner's opposite qualities in herself. Each woman found the other's fully exposed skin color to be a stimulus sunny and shady coming together in a lustrous mixture. Their dark and blue eyes now also produced a blend of their own as they looked fondly at each other.

For now, the pair seemed to be in love. Haverstraw, for one, had already alluded to this above in a sign of his male jealously or even voyeurism? What about the pair's other loves, notably Jacques Moreau and Haverstraw himself for Claudette? That remained to be worked out in Claudette's own mind and in her own way. She as yet felt no conflict, much less any sense of guilt or sin. Eugènie's cautionary talks with her daughter before her departure from Paris receded farther and farther into the past.

The couple, obviously, was now sleeping together. Their affectionate hugs had become closer embraces.

A question then presented itself. Would their intimate involvement in private complicate their situation in public? Even if it didn't, would they feel self-conscious and thus give themselves away? If so, would a backlash against them as a perceived lesbian couple put them in peril when added to their coloring and foreign traits? After all, the inland areas of New Jersey and Pennsylvania where they were headed might *not*, even by the standards of their day, be open-minded enough to accept a pair of their kind. In the midst of people with strong bias or prejudice, even against big city morals and manners, such behavior and appearance held risks.

• • •

In that age even a cosmopolitan urban center like New York City was not as liberal in its racial and sexual mores as was Paris, or France, more generally. French history was full of the licentious escapades of its leaders that extended through-out the populace. Internationalism was then even more evident there than in New York. A wide diversity of cultures, customs, and languages crisscrossed French boundaries via many countries and colonies, including

71

Morocco. To be sure, both women spoke good French in France, not sticking out linguistically as in America. In some places, their foreign status drew attention away from the color issues potentially debarring them.

In France during their period, both women were no doubt aware, as were many others in and out of the arts, of the lesbianism of Gertrude Stein and her partner Alice Toklas, who were subjects of wide notoriety. Small wonder that Gertrude conducted her openly singular lifestyle in France rather than in her native America.

In New York, prejudice could also rear itself as when a regular dancing couple might look away or askance upon seeing a mixed-color or same-sex pair in a Harlem speakeasy *even* in places where they were not banned. Even the Village in lower Manhattan was not yet attuned to open expressions of the kind being described here. Claudette, Dominique, and their friends had to be careful not to incite suspicions, antagonisms, or reprisals.

The Feminist Movement did, nevertheless, help change attitudes along a broad front, moving away from straight laced Victorian attitudes on such matters about women. Artistic social circles were usually quicker to change, even though public morals were not so ready to follow. Even so, France never had to deal with the staid puritan mentality that America, and even New York, traditionally had to contend with.

• • •

Claudette wrote again to Eugènie: "When Dominique and I in New York began to let down our guard on racial and sexual matters, some people began to question us who didn't before. With some exceptions, segregation remains the norm in New York for anyone with obvious African ancestry. This prevails in nightclubs, housing, and elsewhere. This applies to women the same as men. The feminine movement hasn't done much to change that. Any suggestion of mixed-race or mixed-sex involvements is taboo. We'll have to be even more careful traveling outside New York."

Eugènie wrote back at length: "I agree that mixing sexual and racial taboos over there is a risky matter. Please—be more careful. As they say, 'If you can't be good, at least be careful.'

"I've been reading with interest Eubie Blake's *Shuffle Along*. It's a black musical comedy from 1921. It was so popular for white audiences that the same theater set aside a separate hall where blacks could enjoy it, too. That shows how segregation can sometimes be stretched but not usually broken."

She wrote on: "Blacks, I hear, can enter black establishments where whites are also admitted, but they usually cannot enter white establishments. The same is normally true for mulattos; but if they're light-skinned like Dominique, and can enter undetected, that's do-able yet risky. A few white New York speakeasies let anyone in at night where it's dark and there's no trouble. Doesn't all that also explain how John Haverstraw's darker friends occasionally go with him and you?

"Just be careful, dear, especially about dancing with Dominique. Avoid any racial backlash from angry whites against John—taking his black and white friends into night spots supposedly open to all, or even into black night spots that admit whites as well. Messy business: Since segregation exists outside of New York, maybe even stronger, be careful there, too."

• • •

73

Taking her own slant on liberated female sexuality, Dominique asked a trusted co-worker in her store: "Tell me more about Cleopatra, Naguib." It so happened that Naguib Mahfuz was an Egyptian studying at N.Y.U. and interested in his country's ancient history. One day when he spoke about Cleopatra, Dominique picked up on it. It turned out that his good friend, Fatima Sohrabi, herself Middle Eastern, shared a fascination with Cleopatra. Naguib suggested the three get together sometime after work, which they soon did.

"It's nice we share an interest in our southern Mediterranean background," said Fatima. She seemed to sense why Dominique was interested in Cleopatra but did not say so or get too specific on the connection.

After a few initial generalities and pleasantries, Fatima remarked: "I've read about the debate over whether Cleopatra was part black."

"I've read about that, too," remarked Naguib. "How so?" asked Dominique.

"My country's ancient records aren't really clear about this," he went on, "and there are no reliable eyewitnesses; but various later writers and artists depicted her as part black. Shakespeare called her complexion 'tawny'—beige, tanned, or brownish, but perhaps hard to tell if mulatto or Mediterranean."

"Cleopatra," added Fatima, "has since been regarded as an attractive but elusive 'mystery woman,' in part because of her darker skin, not stigmatized as a mulatto…"

"…as she might have been in America today?" queried Dominique.

"Her family's genetic and genealogical make-up," continued Naguib, "is mostly uncertain or unknown. Yes, there was much opportunity for intermixing."

Said Dominique, "Egypt is closely connected with black Africa, but is also white Caucasian, as is much of the Middle East along with Arabic countries. So if someone from over there is darker skinned than others over there, it doesn't necessarily mean that she or he is black or part black."

"Exactly," agreed Fatima. "But many people don't know this and assume a part-black mulatto."

"Let's relate this to the American female movement of today," said Dominique.

"That's a good point," again agreed Fatima. "Naguib?" both women asked, as they looked at him.

"You may be asking the wrong person about that," he began, "but I suppose Cleopatra was one of history's earliest and most celebrated examples of a liberated dominant woman ahead of her time."

"How so?" they asked.

"Just the fact that she was later assumed by many to be part black, and yet was regarded so well, could be used as an antidote for today's feminists who are white but don't yet accept black women into their ranks. Her power as queen, aside from her image, is another matter."

"Well put," replied Dominique. "If a woman like Cleopatra today were part black and yet had a way to get around it by using her Mediterranean background as a disguise, such a woman might still wish to be better accepted like Cleopatra."

"Yes," said Fatima. "She was ruler of Egypt, successful as well as powerful, even if in the end she met a cruel fate."

"She was lover to Julius Caesar," remarked Naguib, "and so many others." She was a Ptolemaic Macedonian Greek who had lots of other diverse lovers as did her ruling family before her. *And* she was *not* 'segregated' or stigmatized for her color."

"Could a part-black woman of today ever become an American president?" asked Dominique. "I've even heard that some of Thomas Jefferson's white contemporaries accused him of having mulatto kids from one of his female slaves."

"Meaning that someday color, gender, race, or other such orientations wouldn't matter any longer?" asked Fatima. "Jefferson's South today has the Ku Klux Klan to punish interracial sex and marriage."

No one really responded.

75

"Or were many ancient Egyptian women more sexually progressive and liberated than females in America today?" asked Dominique.

Again not much response.

Noted Fatima, "Don't forget others like Nefertiti and Nefertari."

The little group then left the coffee shop. Outside, Fatima and Naguib wished Dominique well. For she was about to take a temporary leave for a trip with Claudette down through New Jersey to Pennsylvania.

"Take Cleopatra with you, mystery woman," exclaimed Fatima, leaving Dominique to wonder if that was a come-on.

All smiled as they went their separate ways.

13. Down the Jersey Coast

The excitement of their unfolding scenic American adventure now entered a new episode for the two young women. They had already explored the waterways south of Manhattan leading out along sandy reefs and barrier islands toward open seas beyond. Stirring vistas had opened up. On one side northeast lay the city, looking on over to Long Island. On the other side southwest lay the Sandy Hook area and points further out. The pair now intended to travel south along the Jersey coast as first leg on their extended vacation from their jobs. Their contacts at the small private marina at the tip of lower Manhattan had previously equipped their scenic day excursions close by, and now supplied larger help.

With their sketchbooks and artist supplies in shoulder bags, Claudette and Dominique departed in their friend Maurice's car for Forked River. There the Hensle family from Toms River kept a garvey, a flat-bottom bay boat—at the local river marina. The garvey with its keeper, Bud, was ready and waiting at the dock. His unshaven craggy complexion and loosely fitting cap were as rugged and yet natural as the bay boat he was operating. The engine's chugging sounds and the diesel fuel's pungent smells signaled a new, earthier world of experience lying ahead, different from what Manhattan offered. Salt of the earth.

Out, diagonally down across Barnegat Bay, they went to "Sedge," the Hensle's small private island with a weekend house, just up from Barnegat Lighthouse. The celebrated old Lighthouse stands on the northern end of Long Beach Island across Barnegat Inlet from the southern tip of the peninsula extending south from Bay Head. Aptly named because of the maze of low-lying green isles of sedge all around that whole bay area, the house still provides sweeping vistas for artists. There the pair stayed a short time, adding to their collection of drawings for later use in oils or watercolors, as well as etchings.

From there, Bud gave them another garvey ride over to the nearby town called Barnegat Light, now solitary in off-season. There, they were put in touch with the proprietor of a small hotel where they briefly stayed. Drawing again upon their talents and the scenery, they made further entries into their sketchbooks. A local art group added to their portable art supplies for use on the island in more colorful renderings.

Already the two women were feeling the loneliness of their new environs. Very different was all this from their accustomed ventures and surroundings in the cosmopolitan centers of Paris and New York. These Jersey locales seemed so isolated, even forbidding, despite their beautiful landscapes and seascapes. The usual off-season, or pre-season, depopulation heightened these qualities for the two. Claudette's inner quests were coming more to the fore. Soon the women went off again to explore the island, unfazed by the impending influx of summer vacationers a few months ahead.

One day the two were dropped off at Ship Bottom by another hotel guest. It was near the spot where the very long vehicular causeway stretches over from the island to the mainland at Manahawkin. Here, in the middle of the island, the main north–south road goes from Barnegat Light down to Beach Haven. At that time, the old causeway stirred the imagination with its multiple series of different creaky bridges interspersed with strips of land, all projecting unevenly across the bay's immensity.

This complex setting required an artist's eye to capture it well. Fortunately, sketchbooks were kept in good supply in their ever-present lighter valises. For the more neophyte Dominique, the surface mixture of bay, boats, bridges, buildings, and background challenged her ability to achieve an accurate overall depiction. For the more experienced Claudette, the lonely causeway energized the whole scene. She saw it thrusting its sketchy "impressions" out across the bay toward an uncertain but beckoning horizon, which hovered precariously and indistinctly over the distant mainland, whither she would soon go. Realistic *nature* seemed to imitate Impressionist *art*. Like Claudette herself, the causeway was awaiting the busier traffic of seasons to come. The pair's stop was brief, but long enough to sketch for future oils or watercolors. And also to point up their Realist–Impressionist difference—or perhaps a Renoir–Monet dichotomy within Impressionism.

• • •

As they walked farther down through Ship Bottom, Claudette kept trying to remember the name of the side street recalled by her mother from accounts by Claudette's father. When he was young, he and his family spent summer vacations there in a remodeled old Coast Guard station. After a while the pair came upon it, the name now recognized by Claudette. But which house on that street was it? Basically a block long, the short street, leading on up to the beachfront, had only one real possibility. It was a long narrow frame structure that, as it turned out, had once been located just back from the beachfront, but later been moved back a ways. It bore all the traces of many years of patient neglect. The paint was flaking, the roof shingles curling up, a couple of shutters hung loose.

Agreeing that the worst that could happen would be to be turned away, they knocked on the door. After a long wait, the door opened to disclose a fat, old lady.

"Waddaya want?" she said.

Looking at this creature more carefully, Claudette realized she was scarcely forty, and her white hair was actually pale blond. Her garment (one hesitated to dignify it by calling it a dress) would have hung from her frame shapelessly were it not for the lumps of flesh, like rising dough, that protruded here and there. She wore no make-up, and her hair looked as though she styled it with an eggbeater. Scarcely had Claudette fully framed her first question than the creature said, "We don't know nothin' about any o'that."

Claudette could almost taste the rejection emanating from the woman when a thin man appeared next to her. "What's the problem, Eunice?" he said.

"I'll take care of it, Zeke," she said, but the man turned to the girls and asked what they wanted. Claudette began all over again, but she hadn't even finished one question when his face lit up in a happy smile.

"You girls French?" he said. They admitted as much.

"From France?" he added, presumably just to nail down this essential fact. They agreed again.

It was like the return of the prodigal. He swept them into the building and bade Eunice put out a luncheon for them. With more salt of the earth.

"Now, Zeke," she protested, but he cut her off.

"Make these lovely girls some lunch, woman," he said in a low voice that brooked no contradiction. The girls looked on in some puzzlement but could not turn down a free meal.

•••

Ezekiel Philips never talked to his wife (or anyone else, for that matter) about his experiences as a doughboy in the late war. It had been a terrible time, and he mostly tried to bury it as deep in the past as he could shove it. The worst part of it all had been a few days when he somehow got separated from his company and found himself in a deserted field somewhere in France with the *Boche* after him. Stumbling over one last hill, he came upon a lonely farmhouse. When the French family there found that he was an American, they took him to their hearts, fed him the best food he'd ever eaten (even though it mostly consisted of root vegetables), and, when the Germans showed up searching for him, hid him in a false closet under the eaves.

Soon thereafter his company found him, and soon after that the war was over and he came back to New Jersey, which he hoped never to leave again. But in his mind, he owed a debt of gratitude to anyone from France, a debt so big he could never repay it in full in this life.

• • •

Over a luncheon that turned out to be unexpectedly delicious, the Philips couple, living in this curious building year-round, explained that the downstairs front bedroom was still called the Captain's Room. In the living room, ceiling hooks were still in place for hanging seamen's equipment. It had once been the boat room, its big doors now walled in by the modern frame structure. Upstairs was still the bunkroom; a number of single bunkbeds, still there, were built into the walls on opposite sides of the room, over which were half windows looking out overhead.

The outcome of a wide-ranging conversation was that the two Frenchwomen were invited to stay for a time in two of those single bunk-beds. The Philips husband and wife who owned the house had never traveled, except for Zeke's war experience. They were fascinated by the ladies' adventures as foreigners—which as usual seemed to explain Dominique's "Mediterranean" coloring.

The Philips' son, who worked in a local gas station, retrieved the ladies' belongings from the hotel in the town of Barnegat Light. Claudette and Monique didn't know what to make of this creature. First of all, they assumed that like the rest of humanity he had a name, but they never once heard him addressed by it. When they politely asked what they should call him, he answered "Oh, just call me. I'll know who you mean." His parents were more than generous with his time, repeatedly telling the girls that "the boy will do" this or that errand they needed run.

In most respects, the boy had clearly outgrown boyhood. He seemed to be at least 20 years old, possibly as much as 25 and the girls inferred from various comments that he had

81

dropped out of or been thrown out of a regional teacher's college. He was taller than his father and skinny as a lath, with his mother's ash blond hair and pale blue eyes. He had a way of looking at Monique that made her decidedly uncomfortable. For that matter, neither of the girls liked him much, but his job at the garage gave him access to cars, and he always seemed willing (if not actually eager) to take them and their gear to painting sites whenever they asked.

He slept in the back bedroom upstairs, just across a short hallway or alcove from the bunk-room. They all shared the bathroom in-between those two rooms, so they were all close to each other. The bunkroom was open at the end where the son entered his back bedroom as well as the bathroom used by all three.

• • •

It was then that the dreams at night started up again for Claudette. They had no doubt been stilled by the frenetic pace of life in New York. The new lonelier precincts of her mind, left free to roam in her father's old summer house, could become haunting. Soon Claudette was speaking about them to Dominique—or Monique, as Claudette usually called her.

"What do these dreams mean, Monique?"

"I'm not sure," Dominique replied, "but ever since we left New York on our vacation down here, you've been calling out at night, sometimes screaming. At Sedge Island, the Barnegat Light Hotel, and now here in your father's old Ship Bottom house, you've seemed increasingly anxious about many things. What dreams are you having?"

"Perhaps the scariest dream is when I'm walking alone in dim light through a deserted city on streets that take me into extensive hulks of dark ruined buildings. It's hard to find exits, although I still manage in the end to do so. I'm searching for someone or something."

"Go on."

82

"At other times, I'm trying to find my way toward someone who needs me or is calling for my help."

"Perhaps those some ones in both dreams are your father?"

"Some other times I'm alone, or with you, Monique, looking for happier scenes to paint. Or I've been making love with you and then remember what mother said about such things before I left for America."

"Like what?"

"Basically, that I should be careful so I don't develop a sense of guilt."

"So that's where you've been coming from! A sense of punishment, perhaps? No need to feel guilt."

"That's an old American puritan idea," explained Claudette. "Remember, my father was part Quaker, part puritan in his ancestry."

"What else?"

"If you must know, I've been having dreams about you, Monique, but not about our sexual relations."

"About what, then?"

"Dreams about your past."

"My past? What about it? You don't know anything about my past except what I've told you."

"About your life in Casablanca before you came to France. Hints that certain persons were after you because of some wrongs committed there. Nothing too clear, though. It's probably all crazy and meaningless."

"Precisely, so let's forget it! No need for you to worry about me, much less to fear for me!"

"O.K.," said Claudette, "so let's get on with our vacation here and move on with things."

• • •

Finding suitable scenes for their sketchbooks, in preparation for oil and watercolor treatments, was not hard there. As they explored beautiful Long Beach Island, offseason, they saw nature as their private classroom for

83

self-instruction. Their expansive seascapes and landscapes were mixing in with glimpses of houses, streets, beachfronts, boats, and other local vignettes. A close-up drawing of early morning fishing boats, landing on the beach and loaded with their nightly catches, was soon completed in bright watercolors and sold to an admiring nearby resident for a suitable sum. Two small manageable oil paintings were also sold to the lady's friend, depicting the old long causeway's multiple connecting bridges leading over to the mainland; it extended out from the fishery by the place where the fishing boats beached after dawn with their catch. Both oil works were a mixture of Impressionist and Realist styles, as were many in Monet's middle years as an artist.

Our two artists were then also able to go to Beach Haven and the southern end of the Island for further scenes intended for etchings and watercolors, which they were then hoping to sell to local residents there. Some locals were intrigued by Claudette's name, which she duly signed on their purchases. In the bright late spring sunshine, Dominique tried as usual not to expose her darker "bronze" limbs and torso, but it was not always easy.

• • •

Along the Jersey shore during this period, going back to the 1880s and ahead to the 1930s, artists were working in impressionist and realist modes, depicting the rich diversity of scenes. From Sandy Hook and Bay Head in the north to Cape May in the south, such artists had relatively good access to supplies and materials, also with venues for displaying and selling their works. Conditions varied but Long Beach Island was a favorite place due to its island-at-sea scenery even if somewhat less equipped than artists colonies at Bay Head and Cape May on the coastal mainland (not to mention at inland places like New Hope over in Bucks County). For now, the pair had reasonably sufficient access to needed, fuller conditions at nearby Barnegat Light and Beach Haven, though Ship Bottom remained their focal point.

Although their works then were often preparatory, for completion in more settled situations, the ladies were able, during their extended stay on Long Beach Island, to finish many works of art for sale. Conditions there were challenging but improved, as time went on, for the creation and sale especially of oil paintings.

In order to work in oil, the artist usually needs either a wood panel, or a stretched canvas, or a canvas board panel. Also, an easel to hold it up. Also, oil paintings that are at all fat (i.e., using thick paint from the tube) can take weeks to dry. This is often a characteristic of Impressionist painting. (Van Gogh used half-inch globs of paint in many of his works; yet Da Vinci was able to keep rolling up and carrying around his *Mona Lisa* oil during multiple stages of creation.) Working around this required shortcuts. The girls also devised supplies to do sketching, water coloring, possibly some pastel or gouache work. They planned, or hoped, to make and sell etchings, although they as yet lacked the fuller facilities to prepare etching plates and to develop the plates after they had been etched, as well as a press on which to print them (or someone with a press to print them). Again, some rudimentary shortcuts were devised. To do all this, they would need a car as well as a place to put and to spread out their fledgling accumulation of equipment. They would need to work on site as well as in studio.

Fortunately, the Philipses were interested enough to let the girls use the unused part of the upstairs bunkroom where they slept—which had an adjoining unused little room at the far end called "the fishbowl," with windows looking out picturesquely on three sides. Plus periodic use of the family car. These facilities were, of course, transitory, subject to uncertain future circumstances, with the expectation of eventual transpositions elsewhere. But all this proved extremely useful for quite some time—helped along by the extra modest "rent."

And Claudette Monet's name recognition was again proving to be a definite asset, artistically speaking, in helping to open doors and ease the way.

• • •

Upon returning early one afternoon from their ventures around Long Beach Island, Claudette and Dominique were having open physical relations while wrapped together, naked, on one of their single bunkbeds. The Philips couple and their son were expected to be out all day. But the son unexpectedly returned home from the nearby gas station. Climbing the stairs to his back room, adjacent to the open bunk room where the naked couple lay unaware, he, transfixed, saw in full view their exposed bodies intertwined.

He watched for a while unnoticed…they eventually arose…consternation followed…

When the son's parents later returned and heard the news, the mother sternly reminded the two young women about existing laws against sodomy and interracial affairs of such kinds (Dominique's mulatto body now fully evident) which were "immoral and sinful." The unfazed dad tried to calm his wife down. Their son hinted that he did not disapprove, nor would the other workers at the gas station. His final indignity was whispering that his buddies there might nevertheless want to satisfy "the common male fantasy of watching two women doing it together, young and pretty," as he put it about "male voyeurism", a sophisticated term for this humble Jersey gas-pump jockey as gleaned from his brush with higher education.

"But wait," the Philips' son soon told the other gas station workers, "there's more. I'm hanging something up here on our office wall next to the nude girlie pictures. It's the dark woman's dildo. I found it in their bed. She told me afterward that she 'only had it available, but didn't use it' on her friend 'for a massage to give needed release.'

Man, they were really embarrassed. Should we go easier on them? A real shocker, huh?"

In his more graphic later description for some of his stock car buddies, the same Philips' son explained: "I just stood there silently, guys, watching the lovers going at it for the longest time with their multiple orgasms. Not a one-shot

86

deal like usually with us guys. We were in full view of each other. But they didn't sense my presence because they were so involved with each other. My strongest impression of their beautiful bodies was how dark the one babe was—probably Negroid—in her full body, compared to the whiter girl. Not just bronze or olive, as her head had seemed, but probably mulatto. Eventually they spotted me standing there in the little open hallway between our rooms. Then they jumped up, all flustered, and loudly protested my invasion of their privacy. I apologized and went into my room and shut the door."

"How did *you* feel?"

"I've never seen anything like that. What a show."

The guy's friends said they were "really eating this up." "Tell us more."

Philips' other gossipy exchanges with his garage buddies were earthier and more graphic.

"What did the babes look like?"

"Man, you should see the big knockers on that brown babe. She says to me, 'all we did was mutual masturbation.'"

"Would you believe?"

"The white babe's ass is even hotter stuff."

"Ain't no stoppin' that train now."

"But they best be careful. Lots of tough guys down around these parts."

"So what! Tell 'em we'll pay to see more!"

"Yeah! Pretend we're Phillips 69 gas. This ain't some fancy Phillips 66 station."

• • •

So far, the question of Dominique's color—bronze, olive, or black—had not surfaced outside New York. In these conservative Jersey areas, blacks were far less visible. The Philips parents had once or twice expressed suspicions but then dismissed them as unfounded. Their son now brought up the issue squarely—although he was more

87

concerned with sex than with color, after seeing the two fully naked bodies lying wrapped together in bed.

The two women had planned, if seriously questioned during their travels, to say that the one was the other's maid; but that scheme was now out of question here. Fortunately, a potentially nasty situation was forestalled for the pair by the idiosyncrasies of the Philips family. But they again realized they needed to be more cautious in case their last-ditch cover-up might still be needed in outposts far less tolerant than expected.

Perhaps, around some people, Dominique's image as a bronze or black Venus was her best defense from suspicion she was mulatto, someone to be shunned by others in that segregated era.

In this sense of overcoming adversity and coming into her own, Dominique might be the real heroine of this story—with Claudette's help. What Claudette had always seen in Dominique was often shining through to others in her physique and personality. Yet hot-button issues were again being raised.

The Philips husband still remained hospitable enough toward the girls, and quieted down his wife's mumblings about a she-devil or temptress bringing divine punishment for sins. His wife had enough to cope with already with her jockey-in-the-saddle son. But now this. . . . She spoke about her pastor's sermons on Billy Sunday's popular revivalist preachings on his change from baseball player to evangelist after hearing about Jonathan Edwards' *Sinners in the Hands of an Angry God,* among other influences. Eventually Eunice did calm down. But...

• • •

Things were uneasy at the Philips' place. The parents had been happy to have the two women, including the modest fees received, but complications of race and sex had entered the equation. After some time, the pair decided it best to move on.

88

This turn of events left some uncertainties. The two women had already been planning to explore the natural beauties of Cape May County. Yet the question of transportation now pressed upon them. Fortunately, the older couple prevailed upon one of their nearby friends to drive them there, and they let the young pair keep their belongings there until new suitable conditions were found.

Lodging for Claudette and Dominique proved satisfactory, if temporary, in Cape May. There they found a small but dedicated art colony, through which they soon were seeing notable sights and scenes for their work.

• • •

At the southern tip of mainland New Jersey, largely surrounded as a peninsula by water, they were next door to the southern state of Delaware, with all its conservative prejudices prevalent then, along with those of neighboring Maryland. A kind of unspoken conservative conformity was felt by the pair. Ruins of former houses and streets had been left by slowly encroaching water levels over the years there at Jersey's southernmost tip. The desolate ruins brought back for Claudette her periodic dreams of walking into streets of deserted hulks of ruined larger buildings. Even more evocative were the haunting ghost towns of the Jersey Pine Barrens, where houses, businesses, and mills once thrived but were later abandoned.

Even with her close partner at her side, Claudette felt vulnerable, still needing to find resolution to her quest for her father. The two women with foreign accents and of different coloring still felt conspicuous, even more than they often really were. A lonely complex had settled in over.

Claudette in particular, like the hazy Monet horizon she had seen hovering bayside over the causeway. Looking out across the open ocean from Cape May's southern tip, she nevertheless saw beach dunes and jetties as ideal promontories upon which her artistic imagination and psychological visage could take flight. The Atlantic City boardwalk briefly offered them other projections from which to launch quick sketches for future paintings.

All in all, their extended impressions of the Cape May area conveyed its rich diversity of further coastal scenery. This included glimpses of beaches, dunes, surf, boats, harbors, jetties, fishing, meadows, still life, season, times of day, coloring, lighting, and horizons, along with people, streets, and structures. Subjects again ripe for impressionist fantasies or more realistic renderings—and again worthy even of the original Monet or other masters in their quest to capture the effects of light on color and form in depictions of nature and everyday life.

14. Visiting Princeton

"By the time we are finally arrived in Princeton," wrote Claudette to her mother, "the late spring foliage has been in full bloom at the university and through-out the town and township. The campus greenery is mixed in with the Gothic and other revival styles of architectures. The idyllic scenes are worthy of our best French landscape painters in the impressionist and realist schools. At the university, the extensive special gardens behind the president's house, Prospect, and alongside the dean of the graduate school's residence invite worthy comparisons with Monet's gardens at Giverny. Even more so, in the town, do the gardens at Marquand Park and at the governor's house, Morven. The surrounding areas offer so many expansive lawns and gardens, woods and streams, throughways and towers for our art work. We scarcely know where to begin. Fortunately we have made several good contacts through the guest house where we have been staying. So we've learned rather quickly where and what to focus upon. You were right once again—my name has opened doors for us, with few questions asked.

"Yet I still feel so anxious about many things," Claudette later continued. "Daddy's whereabouts haunts me more and more, with more fearful dreams. Where, still, do I distinguish reality from fantasy, as if in a sketchy impressionist dream world by Monet? Jacques' coming to New York to find me is ominous. John (Jack) Haverstraw says Jacques may be teaming up with Rebecca's black or mulatto friend to track down Dominique, whose past has also been a big question mark in my dreams. I feel guilty

91

about our relationship. I also still feel a little guilty in various ways about my name. But more later."

The beautiful backdrop was becoming yet another Monet-like painting to mask Claudette's inner turmoil. If it was a soothing sedative, it was also one needing careful supervision lest an over-dose give a false sense of reality about what was going on. To deal squarely with one's problems is sometimes better than escaping from them into a false sense of security and well-being. Her painting helped ease her pain. Or was it also the pungent chemical additives like lead that were also at work back then to produce an addictive state of mind as if almost drug-induced?

Claudette's mounting anxiety over her father's fate began to show as she drew closer to his old home areas. "We are sorry to inform you," reported the university records office, "that we have had no contact with alumnus Jack Hornsby in well over two decades. He has apparently dropped from sight." The Town Clerk's Office reported that "a person named Jack Hornsby lived on the Lawrenceville Road nearly twenty years ago, but we have no trace of him here since then." What Claudette had felt would produce a promising lead finding distant cousins living in Princeton and closer to Trenton—also proved to be a dead end. One cousin through marriage had had no contact with Jack over that same long period but once heard that Jack had moved back to Bucks County where he grew up. No further details were available.

As a last resort here, Claudette walked out alone along the lengthy Lawrenceville Road hoping to find the spot where she thought her father's last-known residence was located. What she saw when she got there seemed almost surreal. "If dreams can ever prove real in this way," she later told Dominique, "there it was—the same house I used to dream about; where I saw a man in the circular driveway who later walked into his dining room, with him and others sitting around the table. Does this make me clairvoyant?"

"What happened then?" asked Dominique.

"I was so distraught when I knocked this time at the door in the late afternoon," replied Claudette, "that when the door opened, I fainted and fell on the floor. They called an ambulance, and I was taken to the hospital, treated, and released. My eyes were said, in the hospital report, to be consistent with mild drug overdose, but not sufficient for further action."

"My dear Claudette," said Dominique, hugging her closely. "But you do need professional help. Did the person in that house ever hear of Jack Hornsby?"

"No," replied Claudette tearfully.

• • •

As it turned out, a university student who had helped show them around the campus shortly after their arrival was a senior in the psychology department. He fortunately arranged, through the department's resident Greek secretary, Sophia, for Claudette to have several visits for professional consultation with the senior professor and chairman, a meticulous German.

"Yes," Dr. Bergfeld replied to Claudette's question, "strong chemicals in today's unregulated painting supplies can impair the minds of some people with repeated inhalation. You might want to stop using them too much."

"How much is too much?" She was worried about the new strong art chemicals available in town, not to mention her earlier ones.

"Well, the hospital report you have showed me is consistent with mild drug overdose." He went on to add that "Claude Monet reputedly suffered from eye cataracts due partly to his lead-based paints."

"What do I do? I could never give up painting. It's become my whole identity. But I often feel so desperate—with or especially without the painting chemicals I seem to be breathing in. I worry that the lead that's still added to some oil paints can cause or aggravate serious physical and mental impairments. The unbanned lead base is still good for bringing out whites and other light colors, just as they did for the Impressionists. Look at Monet and Van Gogh. But what about its side effects on the one's poor vision and the other's weak mentality?"

"Why otherwise are you so desperate much of the time? About what else?"

"Mainly about my American father who suddenly left my mother and me in France, never to be heard from again. I was so young, so vulnerable, and really feeling hurt. Mother calls it my wounded inner child."

"I see. What else?"

"I have fears of different people coming after me. I have bad dreams and never know their meaning—whether in fantasy or reality. I'm here in America to find out anything I can about dad's whereabouts, yet fears and doubts trouble me. Nothing seems to be working out the way I hoped." The professor, a doctor of psychology, then talked for a while about the subconscious self and the sense of identity. "The problem of your wounded inner child is coming to the fore. How to treat it is a subject we can go into more detail next time, along with your dreams and fantasies. I know it can be painful, but it can be treated."

"I feel so guilty about many things, including my love affair with my companion traveling with me here in America. In Ship Bottom, our nude sexual activity was called a serious mental illness by some. Is that still a true common medical view today?"

"That, too, can be a subject for further consultation and observation. But unfortunately yes, that is a common diagnosis. For now I recommend you try to cut back on any harmful chemicals or stressful entanglements."

"Maybe you're right, doctor. My friend Dominique says she once read that France's great Napoleon the First died from toxic chemicals in the wallpaper in the place where he lived in exile on the island of St. Helena. That's off the western coast of Africa, well south of her Morocco."

"I have read that, too," the doctor replied. "Thank you for your help, Dr. Bergfeld."

94

"Our accents have gone well together. Feel at ease over here about yours."

• • •

Back to her painting and chemicals soon went Claudette. They seemed again to give her inner peace even if also further anxieties needing to be overcome. Her best form of escape was also her best form of talent.

Claudette and Dominique—their tour guide and art materials in hand—went to the old Princeton battlefield at the western edge of town. The picturesque open site had long included a huge oak tree alongside modern Mercer Road, parallel to modern Lawrenceville Road (where Claudette again felt more vibes from her father's presence). There, General Washington defeated the British troops in early January 1777.

The Park official conducting the tour explained what happened. "Washington and his troops had come back from Trenton with the British in hot pursuit. He went on toward Nassau Hall on the Campus. But he then doubled back to engage the main British contingent in the open expanse of land around the oak tree. Washington won and went on to Nassau Hall. Storming in and driving out the British occupiers, he effectively ended the Battle of Princeton."

"How did Washington do it, against all odds and greatly outnumbered?" asked Dominique. "The enemy was forever chasing him."

"Sheer greatness of character, ability, and determination," replied the guide. "This was one of the few battles during the Revolution that he actually won; but he did eventually win the war."

"An inspiration and example for all of us still today," remarked Dominique.

"Yes, indeed," seconded Claudette.

The two ladies soon ventured forth, over a number of days, to paint and draw scenes there and nearby: fields, woodlands, gardens, streams, bridges, cemeteries, and roads

95

(including steadfast "Battle Road" along Washington's route into Princeton). They sold various impromptu depictions to interested people connected with local art leagues. They had also been planning to go down along Princeton's Carnegie Lake to make sketches for future oil paintings while the University crew teams were having their practices and races. The low Gothic arcades on the boat house at the near end of the Lake angled perfectly with the nearby stone bridge's corresponding Gothic design. All reflected well in the water.

Good prospects already lay ahead for a longer stay in order to capture picturesque Princeton, to continue Claudette's psychological counseling, and to follow up about her father. But news about her husband, about Rebecca's friend, and about others possibly preparing to find the pair forced them to an untimely abrupt departure.

• • •

During their Princeton stay, the two artists could frequently be seen around the town and campus as they openly drew and painted in broad public view. They were attracting attention, not least through the allure of Claudette's name. Little groups of onlookers gathered around to watch them, helping to generate a number of signed sales. Intrigued bystanders not only watched them work and made some purchases; they prevailed upon the readily obliging pair to give little impromptu talks on Claude Monet and French Impressionism. Local news stories cropped up about them. The following excerpts are pieced together from their talks.

"Impressionism," explained Claudette, "for Claude Monet was a long-evolving series of styles over five to six decades of his career. In Monet's classic early decades of the 1870s and 1880s, he tried to capture specific fleeting moments in time and space. He did so by 'manipulating' light, shadow, form, color, focal point, and dimension. Using 2-D by flattening background and foreground closer together, he was influenced by Japanese art prints. He

96

heightened the immediacy of the fleeting moment being portrayed. Later on, he used other techniques such as disappearing horizons. Monet's broken brush strokes remained key to his stylistic 'impressions.'

"Like our master, we seek to capture fleeting moments and transitory 'impressions.' Here these might be scenes along Nassau Street, people gathered in Marquand Park, sporting events in Palmer Stadium, and so forth."

"Let's remember," added Dominique, "that Monet was in ways a realist when rendering the natural details of his gardens at Giverny. In that sense, he was a traditionalist, while also often being an up-to-date modernist, *au courant*. His innovative techniques included his realism in trying to capture transitory moments in time, albeit later somewhat blurred. Fidelity to natural details shows up in the way, for him, sunlight filters through trees or reflects off water. Often his broken sketch-like brush strokes tell the story in such cases."

"By the times," continued Claudette, "when my mother took me to see Giverny through contacts there, Claude's styles had grown somewhat 'abstract.' I prefer his earlier styles, as I think Monique does even more so."

"Tell us what it was like seeing Claude himself in his atelier workshop at Giverny," one onlooker spoke up.

"Well," answered Claudette, "his sizeable house and his large extended family kept him preoccupied. He had one studio inside, later there were two studios, where he finished his paintings of the outdoors. It was a large busy place of operations, which included a half-dozen gardeners. His eyesight when I was there in the late teens and early 1920s was obviously limiting for him. Claude was a personable man. His later paintings reflect this in their very personal and subjective depictions of the natural world at his beloved Giverny gardens."

"Tell us about your intriguing name and relationship to Claude," queried one observer.

"That's a very long story," responded Claudette.

97

"It's a real pleasure having you two young artists visit Princeton," said another admirer.

"The pleasure is all ours. Princeton's natural beauty is justly renowned for its picturesque Monet-like charm. We hope it's never lost in the name of modern development."

• • •

In answer to a bystander's questions about all the supplies and equipment needed for painting and drawing around town, the pair cited their ready availability in Princeton. These included the more unwieldy materials for oil painting chiefly boards, canvas, tacks, and heavier paint chemicals. These were harder to travel with than were simpler, less cumbersome sketchbook materials, as well as watercolors. But their paintings were by now best produced for fairly quick sale, so as to avoid having to lug them from place to place. Fortunately, sales were picking up in Princeton. Intrigue over the name "Claudette Monet," as signed on purchases, helped this along.

"It was an unusual case in point," said a local fellow artist they'd met. She described to another interested group of onlookers in town "how the two Frenchwomen worked with their materials when they rode with me the other day on a freight barge plying the Delaware–Raritan Canal between Princeton's Carnegie Lake and New Brunswick."

"What were they looking for?" asked one. "They were intent to capture the closed, isolated restrictions of towpath life and the expansive openness of the everyday world along the Raritan River near Rutgers University."

"What's for sale?" asked another.

"Some of their new art works include more scenes where the canal continues back the other way toward Trenton and the Delaware. They're leaving behind here a number of these and other depictions still available for sale."

15. Onward to Bucks County

By now, Claudette's quest for her painting and her parent had become an odyssey.

The double mission to find her own sense of identity and home seemed about to reach some kind of climax as she and Monique moved onward to Bucks County, Pennsylvania. Here is where she rightly perceived the center and highpoint of American Impressionism to lie, extending out from New Hope's large art colony. Here, too, was where her father had originally come from and where it was rumored he had returned long ago, all centering for her around nearby Morrisville.

Claudette's agitated psyche was now also intensifying in renewed bouts of dreams that sometimes bordered on hallucination. They occasionally carried over into her daytime activities. Reality and illusion were not always clearly separated in her mind. She clearly needed further professional help, but she was not able to get it while effectively on the run.

To make matters more difficult, Claudette's physical relations with Dominique had been cooling down. Their bonds of basic friendship remained intact; but Dominique's unfulfilled needs were causing tensions and distractions.

Dominique, with Claudette, had her own other problems—whether real…or in Claudette's agitated mind, or both. Claudette's husband Jacques and her lover John (Jack) Haverstraw were reportedly, according to secondhand sources in New York, coming to find and dispense with Dominique as their rival for Claudette's attention. The two men were also now thought to be rivals of each other. What to believe?

Into this complex mix entered other perceived yet implausible threats to the two women—further signs of growing mental unreality. The New York mystery man, Rebecca's "consort," still an unnamed shadow, was said to be on the hunt for Dominique. The son of the Philips couple on Long Beach Island, where they had stayed and been exposed, was in turn said to be after Claudette. The color issue for both women had thus far been handled, but what about racial bigotry further inland?

Claudette kept in mind what the Princeton doctor of psychology had told her about her increasing fears of being pursued and tormented. These were "signs of feeling unloved, despised, and abandoned as a child" by the American father she was trying to find. But no solutions had been offered, short of finding her father. Would even that end the pain and identity crisis? Fortunately, Claudette's personal problems had not yet adversely affected her artwork, but her fear of that eventuality weighed on her mind.

Even so, when she and Dominique arrived in Morrisville, across the Delaware River from Trenton, they were enthusiastically accepted into what was there called simply "the Art Colony." The name Claudette Monet brought instant welcome there on the river's scenic edge of lower Bucks County.

The colony members, living in clusters of houses along the way there, were connected in various ways with the Trenton School of Industrial Arts. Hence the wide diversity of their artistic styles and talents, not always like Claudette's own. While staying with some members of the colony, the pair took advantage, as did many of them, of the area's picturesque features, including the site where the colony was situated.

Claudette soon managed to sell more of her signed drawings and watercolors, helping her to carry on even better. She allowed herself to fantasize about how fledgling future masters like Matisse and Picasso sold works early on to Gertrude Stein for ridiculously low prices. Even Van Gogh, she mused, is said never to have sold a painting in his lifetime.

True to form, our engaging and appealing Claudette Monet was already making new friends and contacts. Any moody eccentricities of artistic temperament were usually understood to be just that—nothing neurotic or psychotic. One such understanding person connected with the Morrisville Art Colony was an older man, Miles Devereux. He was also part French, like Claudette, though American-born.

Sensing that the two women would find another bigger art colony further upriver more suitable to their French Impressionist medium, Miles and his Greek wife, Corinthia, took them upriver to New Hope. There they introduced the two to the many artists still active in what was widely respected as "the New Hope Group of Pennsylvania Impressionists." It was reputed to be the leading such group in America, often identified as American Impressionism.

• • •

Also called "the New Hope Circle of Bucks County, Pennsylvania Impressionists," this circle encompassed large New Jersey areas on the opposite, eastern side of the Delaware River. Bigger areas on the western side extended some distance into Pennsylvania. In the early twentieth century, this whole vast landscape was beautifully pristine (and partially remains so). It was forever captured in myriad fashions by the dozens of prominent painters who worked here, especially in the first two decades of the twentieth century, but also well after. Their medium was most typically oil on canvas, but other forms also stood out. Their scenes varied far and wide—from fields, woods, hills, quarries, streams, and canals to houses, barns, towns, bridges, streets, people, and farm animals.

As Miles drove the two Frenchwomen around this New Hope Circle, Corinthia explained that "It is so-called because of the wide circle drawn by the locals on maps of the region, radiating out from New Hope on both sides of the Delaware River." Claudette and Dominique agreed that "this is the most promising territory for Impressionist–Realist mixtures like our own." The two women pointed out that "The French impressionism of Monet and his followers is well adapted by these American impressionists to the requirements of more realistic applications. A combination best captures the full natural beauty of the region's spectrum of details."

The Delaware River, as these excursions showed, passes down into the New Hope Circle starting first, on the Pennsylvania side, at Point Pleasant and, on the New Jersey side, at Byram. The river's energetic sweep proceeds on down to Lumberville, on the Pennsylvania side, and its opposite, in New Jersey, Raven Rock. Much farther down river is Center Bridge in Pennsylvania and its opposite, Stockton, in New Jersey. Below there, lies New Hope itself on the Pennsylvania side and its opposite, Lambertville, in New Jersey. There remains a little territory farther south down through the "Circle." Much more territory lies westward along roads leading away from the Delaware in the general direction southwest toward Philadelphia. Along these ways there were many associations with her father's background for Claudette to explore.

All along the little roads leading back from towns along the river, the little group saw further challenging scenes for depiction. One such road is the Byram–Kingwood Road leading back from Byram on the Jersey side. Another is the road going back from Pennsylvania's Center Bridge. The river roads up and down either side afforded exquisite vistas and details that Claudette and Dominique quickly noted during their drives around with their two new American friends, who knew the whole region well.

Thus, as the new sightseers were finding out, "the New Hope Circle of Pennsylvania Impressionism" covered an expansive panorama. It extends out from Bucks County across the Delaware River to another state and county—to New Jersey and Hunterdon County. Historic towns, like New Hope itself, dot the map around those parts. Just walking the streets could often inspire flights of artistic imagination.

• • •

The Morrisville art colony, where the two Frenchwomen were now staying in the Devereux house, was immediately appreciated for its charm. As Dominique wrote "in confidence" to a "trusted acquaintance" in New York, "It is in itself, perfectly situated, not far from New Hope, ideal for rendering impressionist or realist scenes. It is stretched out in a number of private houses, mainly along upper Crown Street, which curves going uphill to the top where stands historic Penn's Rock. Back down at the foot of that hill, Crown Street intersects with Trenton Avenue, which itself then slopes downward as it crosses over the Delaware Canal and River roughly parallel to Crown. The many hillside backyards up along Crown Street, which overlook the Canal and River, are filled with lots of old vintage trees just down from the dense woods of Graystones Forest or Woods. At the top of Crown, Penn's Rock commemorates William Penn's purchase of woods ("Pennsylvania"). This picturesque Morrisville area has remained partly intact." Dominique continued at some length.

"Adjacent further up and over from Crown Street, where dense primeval forest once stood, a series of Lower Makefield streets (chiefly Tower, Greenway, and Overton) spiral back downhill today toward the canal and river." Their penetrations into the forest have since allowed suggestive access into the wider virgin land still left there when Dominique was writing. Even the dense woods still present on the side of Crown sloping to the canal stirred the imagination until replaced by art colony houses shortly prior to the French women's arrival.

"Leading further downhill there," she added, "Ferry Road crosses the canal while going to the River Road, which leads serenely up along the river to Yardley, New Hope, and beyond. All along the old canal, with its towpath where mules once towed the barges, are still endless scenes for the New Hope Circle and Morrisville art colony."

Dominique concluded her letter by remarking that "I hope my brownish highlights in these woodsy environs won't give me away and stir up racial prejudice against me or call other things into question. My coloring can change with the light and shade—more neutral as in New York City, or more greenish olive as around the expansive lawns at Princeton, or more goldish bronze as at the sunny Jersey shore. But time will tell." Her (shadowy) "trusted New York acquaintance" (whom she did not further describe) obviously knew the real story.

P.S.—I've been reading about the recent discovery of Cleopatra's sister's skeleton, indicating that both were probably partly black North African in addition to white European or Egyptian. So far, at least, my "Mediterranean" complexion and accent have helped as much as hurt racial perceptions of me as simply 'foreign.'"

The person in question was most likely Fatima, who in New York had dubbed Dominique "mystery woman" with Cleopatra's mixed coloring.

• • •

The same "woodsy environs" of the scenic Morrisville art colony were taking a different, troubling turn for Claudette.

The Graystones Forest adjacent to the Art Colony houses on the northeast edge of Morrisville, between upper Crown Street and the Delaware Canal, was not only an inspiration for artists like Claudette; it was also a mirror for her impressionable psyche.

The pristine natural beauty of Graystones provided a symbolic "touchstone" for exploring her father's remote world in eastern Bucks County. Centuries ago, glaciers had

104

left an assortment of rugged rocks and boulders that now sat majestic trees with heavy underbrush. Going back to the days of William Penn were, and still are, specimens of white oak, other ancient oak, hickory, tulip, ash, beech, dogwood, summer sweet, spice-bush, viburnum, magnolia, and much else. These surroundings left Claudette with mixed feelings of strength and vulnerability as she sought to depict them while simultaneously searching for her father. Uncertain conflicts of her present and past seemed mirrored in these perennial natural cycles of decay and rebirth, which still left her with some hope.

A big question for Claudette had become where and how to distinguish between fantasy and reality. Her daydreams and night dreams were intensifying. The Graystones Forest was symptomatic. Her fractured psyche could easily relate to the twisted jumbles of primeval natural beauty harking back to the forest of William Penn on a much larger scale. Reduced, but more extensive in her day than in ours, the forest is still the biggest of its kind in Bucks County. In this unattended, overgrown, yet self-regenerative forest world, Claudette could readily lose herself in an impressionistic dream-like fusion of fantasy and reality. There, the commemorative rock for Penn as a father–founder could merge in her imaginative artistic mind with tributes to Jack Hornsby, both somehow united long ago and now.

Was Claudette Monet here becoming another kind of Hester Prynne, wandering through her village's hallowed forest, enchanted yet forbidding, in search of the object of her quiet affections? Claudette's different personage was typically stopping to convey, with sketchy impressionistic brush strokes, the fragmented allure of these surroundings as remnants of Penn's vast wilderness. Transcendent ideas were transporting her imagination. Art and life were coming ever closer together in fantasy and reality. Was she alone now in this wilderness, wandering by herself, or was she about to meet another?

16. A Sense of Going Home

Claudette's sense of herself as a painter developed further in Bucks County. There, too, beneath the scenic surface, was taking further root her self-identity as the daughter of the long-lost Jack Hornsby. A split-level Monet–Hornsby persona, sometimes dream-like, was also taking shape.

She searched through old city and state records in Morrisville and Doylestown, then in Trenton across the river. The oddly obscured information, however incomplete, enabled her to piece together helpful inconclusive evidence about her father's background and former whereabouts, along with his and her genealogical roots.

Having already tracked down Jack's early homes in Ship Bottom and Princeton, Claudette was homing in on his earliest two houses in Morrisville. Her mother's vague, brief descriptions had been based on his recollections, especially of the one's older historical appearance. With her uncanny clairvoyance thus far, Claudette found an old part-frame, part-stone, house on Maple Avenue, with colonial looks and a high hedge. It had been deserted for some time according to neighbors, who pointed to it on a copy of an old area map from long before her father.

With Dominique's help, Claudette secretly resolved to set up inside, through an unlocked back doorway, and to spend the night. Walking around the deserted rooms, with distant window views of the river farther down the hill, Claudette found her inner turmoil coming quickly to the surface. The creaky old wooden floors interrupting the surrounding silence didn't scare her in her painful loneliness. But they strangely filled her mind with hope that at last she would somehow be reunited with her father. Even if his presence would be just in spirit, she could still hope for the real thing.

• • •

"My wounded inner child that the psychology doctor (and my mother) told me about is really coming to the fore, Monique. We're safe here, aren't we, in the darkness?"

"I think so," her friend hesitatingly replied. "But whatever happens, please try to realize, as your mother has told you, that your father really did love you."

"I feel a great need to be doing this, to find my daddy; but I'm also scared that I'm breaking the law. Will people pursue me and break in to harm us? Have you ever gone back to your old homes in Morocco and found yourself seeking your departed loved ones?"

"Perhaps, but in a different way," answered Dominique. "But I'm happy trying to help or comfort you. I'm happy for you if you're getting a sense of finally going home, dear." They briefly embraced and then lay back in their sleeping bags.

Claudette started to cry a little. "Daddy, please let me find you wherever you are. I'm still your little girl, aren't I? Please tell me you still love me. I feel so alone and hurt without you."

Trying to console Claudette, Dominique said "I told you that this wouldn't be easy, dear. Remember the difficult stories written about going home. Two books written then by Thomas Wolfe could come to mind. Their titles told the story and the dilemma, *Look Homeward, Angel* and *You Can't Go Home Again.*"

Presently Claudette drifted off to sleep, still crying a little. Not long afterward she awoke, sat up, and called out— "Who is it? Who's knocking at the door?" She called out to Dominique, who said she had been dreaming that someone was coming to see her as the two lay there on the living room floor adjacent to, in full view of, the dining room's

107

front entrance. No one was there seeking her. She went back to sleep. Her dreams came back about seeing her father in the driveway and dining room at his Lawrenceville Road house. Also dreams about wandering through deserted hulks of ruined buildings in search of someone, presumably her father.

Dominique kept silent watch over her companion. "Daddy! Daddy! Is it really you? Please don't leave me this time—or ever again!" Now Claudette was calling out loudly, caught up in her father's very presence in the house they were now in—too real, it seemed, to be a dream. Was it an actual spirit, or just a dream, that she was seeing something? Where was unreality ending and reality beginning?

Presently came another knock at the door. This time Claudette screamed out that others were still coming to get her—the same ones now getting closer and immediately at hand. Namely, her husband, her New York friend and lover, and others, now including Dominique herself, emerging from her mysterious Morocco past.

Fearful that neighbors would hear the cries and find the pair, Dominique woke Claudette from her sleep, causing her to shake and sweat. "I saw him, right here. We even talked together a little. He recognized me and was reaching out toward me when the dream ended. In all my past dreams about him, he never truly noticed or related to me, which really hurt. This time I feel a little better."

Dominique responded, "Is your wounded inner child really coming out, this time, finally to feel loved and comforted?"

"No, not yet, really, but having this sense of going physically home, back to his and my roots, helps a lot."

"Maybe you should draw or paint how you're feeling and what you're seeing."

"Perhaps." Claudette drifted back to sleep until morning. The pair then walked back the several blocks to the Devereux's house off Crown Street in the art colony where they had been staying.

• • •

Dominique wondered if Claudette would finally change her name back to Hornsby, in honor of her father, but thereby risk her mother's ire—and her own name-recognition and identity as an artist. After all, Claudette had sometimes asked if it might be punishment for her disloyalty to her father that she was haunted by his abandonment when she was just a little girl.

But Claudette needed proof of Jack's actual residence and presence. Public records, let alone more private ones, lacked information on that question, as well as evidence on her father's fate. Claudette had to play her hunches again. But where to turn? Did her father's family really live at an undesignated house number on Maple Avenue, as closer searching seemed to indicate, when he was a young boy, long before she was born? No present neighbors remembered him or his family or knew of his later whereabouts. Searching for actual evidence of places where her father had lived, whether in the (wild-guess) house where she had just slept or in some other, was proving impossible to find, far from showing where he had gone.

So far, Claudette's intuition had proven remarkably reliable, even if fragmentary (like the one about the Lawrenceville Road house). These had so often come to her in sleeping or even waking dreams. "Some people are that way," she reasoned. So she decided to try another kind of hunch. The Maple Avenue house where she had slept for one night, accompanied by uncertain visions of her father's presence, might still be the correct address, needing her return. She knew what she had to do. This time she would be alone, once again in her sleeping bag on the floor, for as long as it might take. Clairvoyance was becoming exacting work.

• • •

Anxious and uncertain, still alone, Claudette lay awake for several hours, unable to fall asleep. When she finally did, nothing seemed to happen, except for the feeling that someone was knocking at the front door near where she was sleeping. Nothing further occurred that night. Upon waking in the morning, she was disappointed but still hopeful. Yet another night passed in similar fashion, with a few more knocks heard in her sleep, but nothing more.

Growing strangely more, rather than less, confident and expectant Claudette once again lay there in the darkness. The knocks came again. The door opened. She stood up. In walked a man. He looked over at her standing there. It was the same man she remembered seeing in the Princeton driveway. He had not noticed her there then on the road out front. Nor had he done so even when she entered and sat down next to him in the empty chair at the dinner table. As that man now entered, Claudette asked, "Daddy?" He nodded, "Claudette?" and walked across the room to embrace her. She wept softly, speechless.

Accompanying the man was a little girl. It was the same little girl Claudette had seen in Princeton. There, the little girl had sat on her father's left at the dining-room table—directly across from Claudette, who sat silently and unseen. This time the little girl, now cognizant, followed the man's lead and walked over to Claudette, embracing her. The three hugged one another, with emotion. "Do you know who this little girl is?" he asked Claudette.

This time Claudette intuitively knew the answer. She was not, as Claudette earlier supposed, a younger half-sister, a rival by another wife, whose existence would make Claudette feel even more deeply hurt and unloved.

"She's me, isn't she—Clarissa Hornsby: my childhood name! Or little Claire: Your nickname for me."

"Yes, dear, she's you—several years older than you were when I left you. I have loved you as her, her as you, here where I grew up and feel at home. You have always remained close to my heart. Please forgive me, dearest. I had so many hard problems to escape from or to work out.

Please forgive me, if you can, Claudette Monet—the new name your mother gave you after I left."

"I forgive you, daddy. I love you, too, so much."

"I have felt so guilty all these years over many things."

"Me, too, daddy. Is it all behind us now?"

Over the years, growing up, Claudette had sometimes imagined him with her as the little girl she was when her father left. But he and she as her later grown-up self had never been together in her sleeping or waking dreams she always imagined her younger self as still the same little girl she now saw standing transformed before her in her father's protective presence. By talking in a caring, nurturing way to the little girl (her own self as inner child), Claudette was helping to heal her own still wounded inner child. The little girl now before her seemed to understand and to respond.

The dream and the night faded out for Claudette in an Impressionistic afterglow, hazy but luminous, with sketchy figurines receding into the distance.

• • •

Claudette never again had, or tried to have, such an experience. It made a deep and lasting impression upon her. It seemed so real, decisive, and salutary. Her life was able to move on, far better than before, taking further root in her father's land. Her distressing visions about him in relation to her appeared to be put aside.

Coming home to one's inner self, or child, has been a theme told in different ways over the centuries. One thinks of the return of Homer's Odysseus, unrecognized after so many years away, to his wife and family. Or the return of the prodigal son to his father and family in Jesus' parable. Or even the misbehaving first Adam cast out of the garden in Genesis and the regenerated last Adam in Revelations. After all, the first Adam was cast out in a dream-like trance, whereas the last Adam appeared in a divine vision.

Whether psychologically, spiritually, or artistically, Claudette's active imagination had come unforgettably alive.

111

Would her private vision somehow inspire her art? Would it help her painter's eye enter still more peacefully into the kind of harmonious ideal worlds captured by the great exemplar after whom she was named?

17. Scenes Along the Delaware River

The expansive tranquility of the Delaware River as it passed down through the enchanted Impressionist New Hope Circle, and farther down through the Morrisville area and beyond, carried ongoing therapeutics for Claudette Monet. Traveling and painting in this whole region of Pennsylvania and New Jersey brought her much inner peace. Her art reflected this mental state, now no longer in such turmoil as before.

In order to better capture this still pristine panorama, Claudette and Dominique ventured up to Point Pleasant, Pennsylvania, opposite Byram on the Jersey side, where they could rent a small boat in which to paddle back down to Morrisville and Trenton. Along the way, with their sketchbooks in hand, they sometimes disembarked and walked around on adjacent roads. Exploring in this fashion brought its reward. Some further sales came later when they turned their sketches into finished watercolors or oil paintings. The pair would have liked to go even higher up the Delaware to Frenchtown or higher up to the Delaware Water Gap—all lying to the north of the New Hope Circle and likewise rich with scenery. But they could not manage the extra trip.

Along the way, the pair took time inland to note old Jersey farmhouses on the Byram– Kingwood Road and old structures in Stockton. The Pennsylvania road leading uphill back away from Center Bridge, across from Stockton, was of interest because Jack Hornsby's Quaker ancestors had at various times lived in a number of houses by the way.

Along the river routes on both sides, the two women had to navigate around various little islands and rapids, each filled with its own picturesque potential. Especially noteworthy to them was Bowman's Hill and Tower, downstream from New Hope on the Pennsylvania side, with challenging Scudder Falls farther down near Yardley.

Naturally, the historic New Hope area posed another special riverside attraction for the two artists. Its changing "impressions" of color along the shoreline, as seen from points farther out in the river's moving currents, were reflections of light reaching over to the ever-dominant natural greenery suspended between the blues overhead and beneath. Green trees seemed caught forever between blue sky and water. The fleeting riverside structures passing by, with their shifting rustic reds, browns, and grays, matched those in town, like the old Perry Mansion with its red and blue Bucks County fieldstone. This summer kaleidoscope of light and color well strikes the painter's eye.

Likewise well captured in their preparatory drawings and subsequent oils on canvas was the unique allure of Washington Crossing, just upstream from Yardley.

• • •

Onwards down to Morrisville and Trenton. Just above the rapids or "falls" under the lower bridge and the railroad bridge, the Assunpink Creek flows into the river. There another famous battle took place shortly after the Old Barracks raid by Washington's troops in late 1776. At the creek, between it and the river, Washington's troops were trapped in a *cul-de-sac*. They finally managed to circle around the British at night and proceed up to Princeton for another historic battle.

Claudette and Dominique found the scene where the creek flows into the river of particular appeal for their *plein aire* artistry. They would soon set up their easels for an extended first stage in their oil-on-canvas creations there. What an excellent location for a commemorative statue, they

114

thought, in addition to another at the Princeton battlefield itself.

From the river's Jersey side, near the Revolution's two dramatic turning-points at the Creek and Barracks, Claudette and Dominique could look across toward Morrisville's Summerseat, headquarters for Washington. Their painters' eyes could clearly see at that same precise turning point in the river's sharp westward curve, a panoramic outstretching of the river's two arms. One was pointing to the right upstream and the other to the left downstream, as if to embrace the General's coming destiny, about to unfold in the middle. Nearby will also soon unfold another kind of river destiny for the two women.

"Could a glacier have pushed its way eastward toward Trenton to portend all this in the river's striking contours or contortions for observers like them?"

"Yes," Claudette was later answered, "the glacier pushed its way here and dropped massive boulders, to form a falls in the river later on. But early American builders took most of the boulders for construction, leaving the rapids there today."

"What a dramatic story for this fateful location," said Dominique, as she and Claudette sketched and painted fantasy scenes of these events.

Across the Delaware from the spot where the Assunpink Creek empties into it stands the Morrisville Dike, built in the mid-1930s to protect against flooding. Apropos, there is a painting on a living room wall in the historic Summerseat mansion showing the view across to Trenton before the dike was constructed. The scene looks over from Delmore Avenue to the Island formed between the river on the far side and the stream from the river's overflow on the near side. Farther over, across the river, lies Trenton in the distance. That painting, with its mixture of Impressionist and Realist elements, could still bear remarkable similarity to earlier treatments by Claudette Monet and Dominique Dupré. It could well have been inspired by their artistic examples, made more noticeable to some at the time by the

115

two ladies' French accents and rhyming last names in small-town America.

Not far downstream from the dike, on the Morrisville side, lay what in those days was an actual beach, periodically inundated by salt water tides pushing up river to the lower bridge below the shallow rapids. The beach was photographed with bathers and boaters in the days before the extended dike was installed. At that point, by the tidal estuary just below the rapids, the pair beached their boat at the downriver facility provided there, where water levels were high enough for paddlers going down the river. It would have been great for the pair to proceed further along the Delaware, from here on down past Bordentown's bluffs and marina, as well as Bristol's beachfronts, toward Philadelphia and even beyond. But time and circumstance could not permit.

Art work done by the pair depicting their lengthy river excursion typically ended up in private local hands around the Morrisville area where the excursion concluded. The Summerseat painting described above offers some leads—a whole subject in itself. Similar private sales had already occurred in the same and surrounding areas, as well as in Princeton and Long Beach Island. Naturally some sales took longer than others, depending on the stages of artistic completion. Claudette, much more so than her partner, was not an expensive leading artist to be ranked today with top-tier artists in that wider New Hope Circle from a century ago. But her story is exceptionally compelling, and sales usually proved resourceful.

• • •

On these latest excursions along the Delaware, where the pair filled their sketchbooks, Dominique sensed that Claudette was quietly meditative. Although Claudette remained her usual energetic self in exploring the river region, she seemed absorbed in her own inner world, perhaps pondering how her extensive sketchbooks could best be turned into paintings or etchings.

116

In fact, Claudette had not told Dominique much about her experience alone overnight in her father's boyhood house on Maple Avenue. Nor did Dominique ask her or press the point. Perhaps she figured that her companion had much to think about for artistry's sake after their latest excursions.

"Would you like some time to yourself, Claudette? We've been seeing so much good material to render into art that maybe we need some private time to reflect."

"Maybe you're right. What do you have in mind?"

"Why don't you stay here in Morrisville with Miles and Corinthia for a few days to work on your artistry?"

"O.K., but what will you do?"

"I'll get a ride back to New Hope to study more of the paintings there in the galleries and exhibitions. Our new art friend, Kurt Weise, will put me up there for a while and show me further around."

"All right, but don't stay away too long. I need you with me to give me perspective on things on my art, my life, and everything."

"Of course, dear," said Dominique.

"Is everything else O.K.?"

"What do you mean?" asked Dominique.

"You know, our physical relations and things," replied Claudette.

"Well, it has been harder for me than for you after you stopped making love with me. Looks like I'm the one who has needed it most. You at least have had your Jacques in Paris and Jack Haverstraw in New York. I haven't had anyone like them. It's been hard for me sometimes to concentrate, but I try to understand. I still adore you as a friend and companion, Claudette, but I hope we can get back together in bed."

"We'll have to see, Monique. Thanks for being open with me. No hard feelings?"

"No."

"Good."

"But it can be difficult."

117

"I'm sorry. Please try to realize that I've become very self-conscious about what others might think if they sense our full relationship. They might try to expose us or even harm us as a couple. Fellow artists are more understanding, especially in New York City and even more so in Paris. The bias in America today is so strong against all sorts of taboos—about race, sex, language, customs, everything. Self-consciousness, guilty feelings, can become a problem...

"And give everything away?"

"Yes. Though maybe it's my father's Puritan-Quaker roots coming out in me."

"Speaking of Jacques and Jack, have you heard more from them and what they're doing about you?"

"No," replied Claudette. "I've been feeling safer and more hidden away from all that here in Bucks County. I should keep more in touch with mother, and be sure she is O.K.; but I sometimes hesitate to tell her my whereabouts and doings in case she slips when she's in touch with others about me."

"I think Corinthia is going to drive me up to New Hope shortly," said Dominique. "So I'll see you in a few days. I won't be too long. She and Miles are so nice to let us stay with them. He says 'Us artists have to stick together—especially the Impressionist ones from France.'"

"Take care. Get them a little gift in New Hope from the two of us."

"Bye, bye. I see we're making our own scenes along the Delaware."

"Yes. Bye, bye." They hugged goodbye.

18. An Unsolved Crime

One morning several days later, Claudette had set up her easel and canvas in the Devereux's hillside backyard, poised with it as it slopes down below Crown Street to the canal and river roughly parallel to Crown. She was painting the view looking across the Delaware. It was a sunny, warm day with visibility improving through a morning mist still lingering but dissipating. Just right for a mixed Impressionist–Realist landscape of the kind so prized by the Bucks County Circle. A perfect gift for Miles and Corinthia, to match their sense of motion and things happening in art, life, and nature.

Claudette was subdued but seemed energized with the freshness of the scene before her. Her sleep that night had been restless, yet she was not clear over what. She half wondered what mood she was trying to convey, whether more brightly Realist or more somberly Impressionistic.

She was busy working directly with oil paints, mixing them from her palette, all well in hand. No need in such a setting for a preliminary drawing, aside from a few quick sketches as she went along. Renewed art supplies fresh from a New Hope store and the Trenton School of Industrial Arts were being put to good use.

Before long a neighbor in the same art colony there dropped by to show Claudette some recent depictions of her in the shadows looking through the tall trees leading down the nearby Crown Heights hillside toward the canal and river including a stately medley of dogwood, maple, white oak, pin oak, birch, American beech, sycamore, and hemlock. "Soon," said the neighbor, "you should exhibit this and your other recent scenes at Summerseat and also in New Hope. Dominique's paintings, too; they're getting so good. Last time at Summerseat you both showed other scenes looking across to the island, the river, and Trenton. Some features were later copied by others as well as me."

"Thank you for the encouragement" came the reply, "and our thanks to Summerseat for some sales."

• • •

Presently the back door opened and Corinthia called Claudette to come over. Puzzled and concerned, Corinthia said that she had just called the New Hope place where she had taken Dominique days earlier. Corinthia was calling there to find out when Dominique wanted to be brought back. Strangely, it turned out, Dominique had not actually stayed there but had wandered off on her own. It was not clear where she had gone or with whom. Dominique was last seen, not long after arriving there, getting into a black Ford coupe (in prototype) and driving off with someone half-hidden by the small tilted frame of the rear window. Nothing more was known. Several days and nights had now elapsed without any sign of her.

The question was what now to do, if anything. Claudette, too, was puzzled and concerned. She suggested that she and Corinthia drive up around New Hope and along the main roads to look for a possible black Ford coupe. Their half-day search proved fruitless, too open-ended and time-consuming. And still no sign of Dominique upon their return. By now, both women were becoming apprehensive. This was not at all like Dominique—just to disappear on her own for days without saying anything about her doings.

But, again, what to do? Following his schedule at Trenton's School of Industrial Arts across the river, Miles was already back at the house upon the ladies' return. Hearing the story, he drove to the New Hope Police Department and looked around some more there, but he came up dry. The police there suggested he call or go to see

120

the police departments in Yardley, Morrisville, and Trenton. After some hours spent doing all that, he still had no leads.

Whose car could Dominique have possibly gotten into, much less without a trace? No Ford coupe crossed Claudette's memory of cars she or the Devereuxs had recently seen. No other friend or acquaintance of hers remembered seeing one either, certainly no one Dominique was likely to take off with in such fashion.

Another day passed. The area police departments were now actively searching for a missing female matching Dominique's description. The hunt was on for the kind of car described. Still nothing.

All sorts of scenarios went racing through Claudette's affrighted mind. Who else could be involved—from France, New York, New Jersey, Pennsylvania, or somewhere nearby? Had anyone from Dominique's recent or remote past caught up with her out of some personal animus? Even someone from Dominique's mysterious past in Morocco? Alone in a foreign country, both women had sometimes been on guard against random acts of violence. Would their gender, language, color, class, or sexual natures have been a factor? Was there yet a reasonable chance for a safe return? Could there have been a bias incident or a crime? A sexual predator? A consensual sex act gone awry, whether with male or with female? In the course of ordinary conversation, various people in Morrisville, Yardley, and New Hope had been told that Dominique was going to New Hope alone for a short stay. Further queries among those people also proved fruitless. Could any of them have inadvertently told someone else, or could the Devereuxs have casually mentioned those plans to others? It seemed not to be the case.

• • •

Then, in an early evening, came a telephone call to the Devereux house from the Trenton Police Department, asking them all to come across the river to the department. Upon their arrival the chief police detective handling the case brought the fearful trio into his office and asked them to sit

121

down. "I regret to inform you," said the detective, somewhat awkwardly, with solemn but gentle countenance, "that there has been a homicide."

"Oh no, oh no," Claudette cried out and began shaking and sobbing. Miles and Corinthia tried ineffectively to console her.

Before the detective could continue, an assisting second detective entered the room and stood at his side. Miles asked "Are you sure who it is?"

"Our preliminary reports indicate that the victim is a mulatto female, age late twenties or thirty, with wallet identification matching information recently conveyed to us by the Morrisville police."

"Oh dear God, help me," cried out Claudette as the second detective tried to console her some more.

"Where is the body, so we can be sure?" asked Corinthia.

"It is being taken to the city morgue. Pending our preliminary coroner's report, you will be able to see and identify the body there very shortly. The medical examiner's office will be assisting you."

"What then?" asked Miles.

"Since the victim was staying with you, you and the victim's close friend sitting here will be asked to fill out a verifying affidavit. After that, the body will be released for burial. Since she is of foreign citizenship, special contact information will be needed."

"But before all that, we want to know what happened," said Miles.

"Of course," responded the chief detective. "This is where we need your help. We have very little forensic information in this case."

"Was it an intended murder?" asked Corinthia. "If so, by whom?"

"Undoubtedly, but no real clues yet. The body appears to have been sexually traumatized, strangled or otherwise asphixiated, and thrown into the river. It floated down to the Trenton area. A fisherman spotted it. We are still not sure where these events took place, or on what side of the river the murder occurred. Not clear yet how the body was dropped, possibly from a bridge. But where the body ended up, across river from your backyard, places it within Trenton police jurisdiction in a criminal investigation."

Specifically, the body was found floating in shallow water near the Trenton Filtration Plant, ominously opposite the Morrisville art colony and just above the upper Calhoun Street Bridge.

After further proceedings along these lines, the sorrowful trio was taken to the Trenton morgue to identify the body. As far as they could tell, it was that of Dominique Dupré, but it was quite battered.

• • •

There continued to be no evident cause or motive for the crime; but a police spokesperson speculated…"There have been some bias-hate crimes in the Trenton Morrisville area in recent times. Unofficial segregation still runs strong. Some whites were angry about negroes moving in. Since the victim was reported to be a close traveling companion of her white friend, with both having heavy foreign accents, it was possibly a crime caused by other forms of racial hatred. Prejudice or passion—it's still not clear. Or it could have been someone from farther out of state, like New York. Some in the New Hope neighborhood where the victim was going, remembered seeing a Ford coupe driving around, possibly with New Jersey or New York plates. Others reported hearing strange inquiries about the pair. Authorities in both states, as well as Pennsylvania, will be questioning some of the French pair's friends and acquaintances there."

Meanwhile, Claudette was asked to describe any and all persons who might have had motive or opportunity for such an act. A number of people were popping into Claudette's mind. "Could it even have been a crime of vengeance by someone from out of the country?" she asked herself. Police will also question Jersey contacts, she was told, in Ship

Bottom, Princeton, and elsewhere. All sorts of far-out connections for information on herself and Dominique were going through her mind, which was still in turmoil. Could even middle-eastern Fatima, or the Greeks, Sophia and Corinthia, or artist Kurt have given unknowing tips to their whereabouts?

"But at this rate," she wondered, "will the case ever be resolved? If not soon, at least in the future? Or could it take more complex cycles of time and circumstance, as do so many other things in my life?"

Claudette now felt more alone than ever. She was adrift from her native land, bereft of her best friend and faithful companion, and hesitant to reconnect with her New York friends, who were now subject to questioning and who would be unavoidable when she might soon return to work. Claudette became more aware than ever of how much Dominique had meant to her. Who or what else to turn to? As if in a Monet painting, would the Impressionist shadows around her ultimately reclaim her form, as they had done with many more shadowy unfinished figures in her own life's "fantasy sketch"?

19. Trials on a Spiritual Journey

The mystery surrounding that last question brought Claudette back again to the ultimate one—her father's whereabouts, living or dead. By now, it seemed to her, her searches had exhausted every possibility. Where could he have been all these years—and decades? In her present grief and loneliness without Dominique, and remembering the deep solace she derived from her vision of her father, Claudette now resolved to make one last effort to track him down. But where to look now?

It then occurred again to her that her father's family had various Quaker roots. Perhaps they would furnish a lead to him if she could track them down. She contacted the Quaker meeting-houses in Princeton and Trenton, without results. Then she searched Bucks County, traditionally a central Quaker area, for Quaker meetinghouses that might have information. One was the sizable community in Buckingham/Lahaska. Again no success. Like most Friends meetinghouses, each of these had an adjacent cemetery usually backed up with accurate records. But still no leads.

In these searches, Claudette soon learned that during certain earlier periods in their history, Quakers had buried their dead without grave markers. Their belief was typically centered on the Universal Spirit, with which the deceased would be united, needing no special grave markers. In these cemeteries some areas had markers and others did not. In the latter cases, bodies were often buried next to each other in a common grave, even though corresponding meetinghouse records would still be kept on who was buried there but not precisely where. In any case, burials of more recent periods

125

were typically, but not always, marked in some way, whereas those of certain earlier historic periods were often *not* marked. This meant that if Claudette's father was buried in a Quaker cemetery, his burial site would likely have, though not necessarily, a marker, as well as corresponding information in the record books.

• • •

Suddenly, at another such place, and in quick flashes, Claudette was severely jolted. There he was, her father, amid dozens of unfamiliar names in a yellowing ledger. Calling out, "Daddy! No!" she was all alone there for the eternal moment of truth. Claudette resisted the end of hope that they would see each other again. Just as quickly she then realized and accepted, prepared by now, that here indeed, finally, lay her long-lost father. "Daddy! Yes!" At long last her search was over. Her long quest since early childhood—her transatlantic odyssey—might at last have resolved the uncertain ache in her heart, but her longing to unite with his American roots would continue.

The immediacy of this fleeting climactic moment in time seemed frozen forever for Claudette in an eternal consciousness of a higher reality, as if seen through a full Monet lens of changing impressions still alive today.

Jack Hornsby had, in fact, lain for many years in an unmarked burial site, surrounded by other, undesignated persons, in this small Quaker cemetery in Bucks County. The meetinghouse records confirmed his presence there, but not his specific death date. The sequence of entries in the record-book clearly indicated his burial had occurred many years earlier. The current record-keeper said that although such unmarked burials were very uncommon for the modern period of the early twentieth century, they did in fact occur, depending on the deceased person's or family's request. There were, in other burials of the same period, grave sites at that cemetery with appropriate markers.

126

Naturally various questions arose for Claudette. Her initial mixed reactions to her unexpected discovery did bring back her childhood sense of loss and abandonment. "How could Daddy just leave me the way he did?" she asked out loud when taken to the cemetery adjacent to the meetinghouse. "He now forever rests in peace," said the gentle elder who accompanied Claudette. Her wounded soul had long been crying out for love, help, and identity.

"Why would Daddy want to do this?"

"Perhaps," replied the elder, trying to reassure her, "because he felt his own soul could find release by being united with the Universal Spirit in a realm of Universal Peace."

"What else do Quakers believe?"

"We look to the Universal Spirit for our answers to the meaning of life and death, but not through material worship or rituals. That's why we have no organized systems of church service or worship. You might like to join us at a Sunday morning meeting. Our members would gladly welcome you."

"Thank you," responded Claudette, and departed for Morrisville, thinking about the Quaker spirit of peace and brotherhood. "If Daddy has found his own peace, harmony, and release, will I ever do so?" she asked herself.

• • •

At the Devereux house, consternation was still the order of the day. Miles and Corinthia were resolute in their support for Claudette, who by now was beginning to fear she might have outworn her welcome. Finding her father's resting place, they hoped, might eventually bring some further closure to her feelings of abandonment. A sense of coming home by being close to Daddy would take time, they acknowledged. Because the older Devereux couple had no children, they were happy to have Claudette's company for now. She and they were easily of an age to be child and parents.

127

Meanwhile, the murder investigation was not leading anywhere. The coroner's final report confirmed and expanded upon the original information. No perpetrator had been identified or apprehended. Thus far, the crime remained unsolved. A cloud of inconclusion remained for Claudette, leaving her to wonder who in her recent past might have done and again do such a thing.

One big item did remain for Claudette, needing the Devereuxs' help: what to do with Dominique's body. All efforts to contact her mother and father in Morocco had come up dry. Something had to be done before too long. Cremation was agreed to be the most sensible route to take, followed by burial somewhere and somehow so as to relieve Claudette or the Devereuxs from having to maintain and care for a bulky urn.

A plan was devised, not the best but perhaps the easiest of difficult alternatives. One night, when the urn carrying Dominique's remains was at last ready Miles and Corinthia drove Claudette over to the meetinghouse graveyard where her father's remains lay undesignated. Because none of them including Dominique herself were members, all permission would have been denied by the members of the meetinghouse to dispose of the ashes there. So the trio had to act in unfortunate stealth, partly hidden by the high brick wall surrounding most, but not all, of the graveyard. In a corner area by the unmarked graves, Corinthia used a garden tool to dig a little hole large enough to bury the ashes and to cover with soil on top. A little ash was left over to place in similar fashion in the Princeton and Trenton Quaker graveyards. The trio then departed, to do the latter on another night. All went reasonably well.

• • •

The real question was how it would be best for Claudette to move on. What should she do, or where should she turn next? No father, no companion, no real prospects for now of a return to New York or to France.

128

Not surprisingly, Claudette once more found refuge in her art. For the time being, she found time and resources to paint pictures, for pleasure and for profit, of Bucks County scenes. She had found a measure of peace and belonging in the Morrisville corner of the extended New Hope Circle within its wider circumference in Pennsylvania and New Jersey. She went on occasion to the meetinghouse cemetery to paint scenes of the place where both her father and Dominique lay buried amid picturesque surroundings just right for inclusion in the Pennsylvania and New Jersey kinds of Impressionist–Realist landscape paintings. So as not to overstay her welcome, she found a nearby place of her own, conducive to her art.

Also, after a long interlude, Claudette was back in touch with her mother in France, even talking to her long-distance by telephone. Eugènie seemed reassured that her former husband's whereabouts had at last been settled. Like the meetinghouse elder, Eugènie urged Claudette to find solace in the knowledge that her father was at peace himself, as he would want his daughter to be at long last.

Looking back on her long spiritual journey thus far, Claudette was learning elsewhere about her real father and mother in a higher sense. She was hearing about her true home and identity as a reflection of a diviner life and love. Finding her inner self was not just a matter of dealing with her "wounded inner child" on a psychological level, however helpful that might be. She would need something more, she was told, to help her deal with life's myriad human imponderables. Would scenarios of victimization, retribution, and so forth need to be put to rest, rather than dwelled upon, if peace of mind was to be found? Coming home to her Father–Mother, God, brings the Comforter, who "will heal . . . thy wounds" (*Isaiah, Jeremiah*). It could bring her "perfection as God's child"—as divine image and reflection.

"How interesting," Claudette said to herself, about this last outlook in relation to Claude Monet's Impressionist vision of present perfection in the natural and human worlds.

129

As captured by the artist, fleeting moments in time are suggestive of more eternal universal truths. In these dream-like states, time merges with eternity, as in Claude's later blurred expansive horizons. There past, present, and future seem suspended in an eternal momentary now. A divine as well as natural reflection often occurs in Claude's scenes of light and sky mirrored off the water and giving off an ideal peaceful beauty. A more transcendent realism was often merged in this fashion by Claude, as Claudette knew, with graphic detail, as in some of his garden scenes. These overall therapeutics were again comforting for Claudette amid the trials on her continuing spiritual journey.

20. Further Flashpoints

Seemingly out of nowhere, as things were settling down, came further flashpoints to disrupt Claudette Monet and others around her. Not long after the final burial of Dominique's remains, a new light was shown on her murder. One morning, a hastily scribbled note was found stuck to the Devereuxs' front door, put there the night before. It read simply: "Your mulatto ["N" word] lesbian foreigner finally got what was coming to her around here. Artsy bitch, anything goes."

Many questions were raised as the threatening note became public knowledge in the small area communities, usually shielded back then. Would this latest development lead to a resolution of the case or to further violence? Did the word "your" signal a new vendetta against Claudette as well as the Devereuxs? Did "around here" refer to perpetrators in the wider Morrisville–Trenton area? How long a period of advance brooding was meant by "finally"? Was the writer either Dominique's killer or someone else with actual knowledge of the crime, or just someone who harbored personal animosity toward blacks and lesbians? How did the writer know about Dominique's color and orientation—from observation of the pair or from hearsay? Had the writer come from somewhere else in Pennsylvania, New Jersey, or New York, using the issue of race and sex to throw suspicions in a different direction? Would the writer know where in Morrisville Claudette was now living and go after her? Would she need to keep on the move again? Had the note's writer seen the open affection between the two women or observed them during their outings on the

Delaware when Dominique's mulatto coloring was more fully noticeable around parts of her light clothing? Or had someone from the Ship Bottom area heard about Dominique's nude mulatto body in bed with Claudette? Was the writer also someone who had heard both women's "foreign" accents and thought them "strange" (apropos the dual term *étrange*)? Or was that last element meant to throw investigators off track?

The note attached to the Devereuxs' front door was promptly taken across river to the same Trenton police who had handled the crime in the first place. They told the shaken trio that there were probably no easy answers to those questions. They cautioned Claudette about her public appearances in the meantime, while further investigations were under way, in case the killer had been lying low and was again on the prowl. For she remained the chief target for vengeance or vendetta.

• • •

Sometimes people at the center or periphery of a crime feed on the publicity about it instead of being scared off. Whatever the case, another scribbled note was soon found attached to the Devereux's front door in the Morrisville art colony. It simply read: "You artsy aliens better watch out— exposing herself and driving around like that." Not only was prejudice against artists now added to the mix of local motives but also garbled allusions to brown bodies, car rides, and not belonging.

The new preliminary statement by the Trenton police as to cause and circumstance read simply: "Probably racial and local motivation, with long-aggravating factors of sex, language, and class, all brought now to a head by the victim's open exposure in warm weather while traveling on the river and painting around town."

Claudette's series of further statements to the police were openly personal and emotional: "During our picturesque last journey down the Delaware, our

132

attractiveness blended well with the surroundings. In the bright sunlight of the season, with light clothing exposing more of our bodies, we were feeling free and easy."

"Dominique's openness," recounted Claudette, "showed her skin coloring to good advantage. Her light bronze or olive Mediterranean shades were fading into a more dominant North African mulatto brown. Obviously Dominique's body was not fully exposed here as at Ship Bottom, when observed in bed by the Philips's son. Otherwise, the mulatto shades would now be even more apparent during our river trip. Dominique's skin coloring added to her bodily attractiveness; slightly sculpted, it fit subtly in with the demeanor of people (often themselves unaware) in the art colonies frequented by us.

"I, Claudette, fully accepted my companion's coloring. I would sometimes remark to Dominique that 'our respective lighter and darker coloring is a natural combination that sets each of us off to our best advantage.'

"Even so, we tried to be conscious and careful in these days about public viewings—which were usually limited to our less obvious head and neck, not legs, waist, arms, or shoulders. We really resented those Philips types and their obscene wisecracks about us two, providing good sexual fantasies for men as well as women."

These statements to the police did not allude to the "driving around like that" by Dominique as mentioned in the second note on the Devereux's door. Not directly party to that last car ride, she remained in the dark, as did the police. What did the phrase mean or prove? Many different angles could be conjectured. Suggestions were welcomed. However tantalizing and lacking resolution, the mystery of why and with whom Dominique got into the car would still remain just that, unless someone came forward with something else at least about the note writer's identity. Not all murders are readily solved, satisfactorily or conveniently, in real life—or in fiction.

"Maybe," said Claudette to the detective, "I don't want to know what happened."

"What do you mean?" asked the detective.

"What if the truth or reality is not pretty more simple and complex than earlier scenarios imagined?"

"How so?"

"Well, in deference to Monique and her situation, I'd like to remember her just the way I do now— happily, as my best friend and loyal companion."

"We'll have to leave it at that for now."

• • •

Like the proverbial animal with many lives to die away and be reborn, this unsolved murder and its reporting were not easily lost from public view, but kept regenerating into further flashpoints. Rumors took on lives of their own, becoming events in themselves for area audiences unaccustomed to such happenings and possible threats of re-happenings left hanging in abeyance. Rumors had a way of feeding more rumors. Area newspapers and radio stations were conducting interviews on the crime, its aftermath, and wider issues of public safety and police effectiveness. For Claudette, the Devereuxs, and others, the uncertainties and insecurities were bound to linger as reports like the following kept reappearing in area newspapers and on radio.

Asked one interviewer, "Why are some people still so upset by this crime? Why do some seem to feel as negative about the victim as about the perpetrator?"

"Let me ask *you* a question," came the response. "Why do you think this murder happened in the first place?"

"What do you mean?"

"Well, let's don't somehow be blaming the police."

"Meaning what?"

"Come on. Everyone knows, or should by now, that some regular people as well as extremists will feel threatened by unwelcome outsiders in their midst who are different and don't belong."

"That sounds like racism."

"Call it what you want. Unofficial segregation is still a fact of life around here. 'Coloreds' as well as 'queers' in this day and age should know their place."

"Go on."

"You can say what you like, but Negroes are getting a little too uppity around here. They walk down the street like they own it and don't get out of the way when I come by. Next thing you know, they'll be marching into Woolworth's and ordering a cup of coffee and a donut."

"And women?"

"They say those two foreign girls were, you know, like that. Not that I really care what people do in their own homes. Their business is their business. But when a couple of foreigners with names no Christian could pronounce without he got drunk first, come over here and start doing it all over the place, I think something needs to be done."

"What else?"

"Look, would you want your property values lowered, your jobs given to lower-paid workers, and your way of life threatened by outsiders like that moving in? It's been happening in other places. Let one in, they all come in. Like dominos falling one after another, with whites moving out and blacks moving in till the whole town is changed."

"But the victim and her friends were just harmless law-abiding artists."

"That's another thing. A bunch of immoral artsy craftsy creeps from New Hope. Let them all stay up there where they fit in better."

"Going around town here with their art stuff, painting scenes out-of-doors is too odd, I suppose? Or does it all come back to a question of racism?"

"Have it your way. Why would they want to be out there anyway, attracting attention to themselves, the one looking like the mulatto she was?"

"Tell me, then, why didn't they have such problems like this when they were in New York or before that in Paris?"

"Don't give us that New York crap down here in this day and age. And who gives a damn about Paris? Is that all now? I have to go."

"O.K. Thank you for your time."

• • •

Another kind of interviewee was more blunt, less articulate.

"What do you think about all this?" came the question from another interviewer.

"Not much" came the reply.

"Meaning what?"

"Meaning we ain't got no room for strange people like that 'round here."

"Can you be more specific?"

"Don't give me no attitude. You newsy liberals think anything goes. That victim combined all the worst."

"Like...?"

"Like mulatto, lesbian, foreigner, immigrant, artsy—you name it, from all us regulars have heard and seen."

"So...?"

"So we's had enough of all dat. We don't want no loose immigrants movin' in around here and no un-segregation in this here day and age."

"I guess that's what it's all about?"

"Reckon so." And so it went.

• • •

Needless to say, these two interviewees were not fully expressive of average citizens in their attitudes there and then; but they seem representative of some people when strongly objecting to such unwelcome outsiders in their midst, through no fault of the police trying their best to cope.

Naturally, over time these personal controversies would subside, hopefully then to be forgotten. But they did not die easily. At least northern segregation's stereotypes—kept by a relatively few diehards about so-called "coloreds and strangers" with unclean bodies and loose morals—did not reach the levels of southern segregation and xenophobia.

Meantime, other voices were being heard in public about ways to get around or overcome the perception, by some, of threats to housing, property, and employment posed by minorities and immigrants. Crime and safety were key topics debated in matters of public policy. Clergymen, as well as politicians, entered the debates. One pastor's public statements related to *The Book of Common Prayer:* "We pray for those who are victims of hate and prejudice and the end of phobias that fuel violence against those who are different." Matters of public morality and sexuality were also debated.

Were these diverse elements tending to divert attention away from outside forces toward more local ones in the unsolved murder of Dominique Dupré? Where did the true balance lie? Was the investigation clouding up or, in fact, clearing up through a combination of outside and local forces?

• • •

By now the lessons Claudette was learning were about the darker sides of life in small-town, not back-town, America in places like the foregoing, especially during the insecure late 1920s and early 1930s. The overwhelmingly white population strictly enforced segregation in housing and employment. Same-sex behavior was taboo. Strong stigmas against immigrants extended widely to foreigners of all sorts. Each of these items could be bad enough by itself; but taken together, along with loose artsy temperament, they could be horrible. Race, sex, and nationality could present a triple threat to one's well-being. Not surprisingly, Dominique had stood out, often to her detriment, becoming a target for loathing and vengeance. She and Claudette had been too easily assuming more liberal New York and Paris to be the norm for inland America. There, racial prejudice combined with class bigotry could still prove obsessive and explosive.

Then again, there was no real evidence, as the investigation unfolded, that the person who scribbled the Morrisville notes was a person from that locale or region. The door was still open that one of the other American or French possibilities in Dominique's or Claudette's background could be culpable. The crime was still unsolved and left open. Would time still reveal anything about Dominique's demise as well as Jack Hornsby's?